Ta Weezo's Blues
By
Layla Dorine

A Desolate Press Production
1120 Main Street
Osage, IA 50461

Cover Art: Rue Volley
Edited by Crossfactor Ink

Dedication: Without the insightful and absolutely amazing conversations with fellow attendees of the Native American Literature Symposium, this story would not exist. Thank you all for welcoming me into your midst, sharing your knowledge and experiences, and creating an atmosphere where learning and discourse are nurtured and celebrated.

Chapter 1

THE HALLWAY SMELLED of old dust and coconut curry, setting Sabre's stomach growling as he trudged the last few feet to Professor Locklear's door. Instinctively, he pulled his hood low, casting a shadow over his eyes, and with practiced ease, he swept his hair forward. It would have to do. Sucking in a deep breath, he counted to five before letting it out slowly, then licked his lips, and knocked on the door.

"Come in!"

The voice was slightly muffled by the wood that Sabre partially shoved open, only enough to poke his head in about halfway.

"Excuse me, professor, do you have a minute?"

Sabre kept his head angled, watching Professor Locklear out of the corner of his eye. Several moments passed before his professor stopped writing and placed the pen beside his notebook, raised his head, adjusted his glasses, checked the clock, and then brushed a stray strand of hair back from where it had fallen over one eye.

"I have a few, so you might as well come in. No sense hovering half in and half out of the doorway."

Sabre shuffled forward, carefully keeping his eyes lowered as much as possible.

"So, what can I help you with? Are you in one of my classes?"

"Yes sir, I'm in your ten o'clock Introduction to Native Literature class."

"Ahh, you must be the one who sits in the corner by the emergency exit, where it's nice and dark. I have to admit, when you first chose that spot, I assumed you were looking for a place to nap, but you've since proved me wrong. Whenever I look your way, you're focused intently on me or the power point."

"Yes, sir. I enjoy the material and some of the discussions are pretty fascinating."

"Really? In that case, why is it that you've never taken part in any of them?"

Shuffling from one foot to the other, Sabre carefully contemplated the question before responding. "I try to let my papers speak for me. I'm bad at public discourse. I get tongue-tied and trip over words or end up being so hesitant that people talk over me. When I'm writing, I can organize my thoughts and present a more complete analysis of what I've read."

"Sounds as if you are extremely self-aware. Not a common trait these days, I'm afraid. Still, if you feel you have something to add to a conversation, then I hope you won't refrain from doing so, er... I'm sorry. You'll have to help me out with your name."

"It's Sabre."

"Ahh, yes, one of the more unique ones this year. You're right; your papers are remarkably organized, well thought out and quite complex in their reasoning. I must admit, you've had me rereading a few things I haven't gone through in years just to understand why you've presented some of your comparisons in the manner in which you've organized them."

Sabre grinned, a surge of pride rushing through him. "Thank you. That's actually why I stopped by. I was wondering if you had any books you could recommend, similar to the required material for the course. I've finished reading everything on the syllabus, plus the referred texts I came across when I was researching; killed a couple piles of sticky notes and pens in the process, too, so now I'm hoping for more."

The professor's eyes went wide and he steepled his hands on the desktop calendar, tapping his fingertips together as he slowly scrutinized Sabre, making him shuffle more and tug at his hoodie to ensure it shadowed his face.

"Try as you might, I don't think you're going to change colors and blend into the woodwork. If you do, I think I'd have to take a half day off and schedule an immediate exam with my optometrist," Professor Locklear remarked with a chuckle. "You can grab a seat, you know. I'm not a fire-breathing dragon about to roast you for stepping into my lair, though I wish I could singe a student or two when I catch them snoring."

Sabre chuckled softly but didn't come any closer.

"I guess not. Well, I must say your question caught me a bit off guard. It's not one I'm used to, at least not from someone who wasn't required to take my class. Are you considering adding Native Studies as a minor? You are a junior, correct?"

"No, sir. I'm a senior."

"Ahh, okay. So are you looking for something specific?"

"Well, I, umm, really enjoyed *Reservation Blues*, so I found the other Sherman Alexie books and read them too. I loved the myths and legends book you assigned, and *Fools Crow* and *Love Medicine* were extremely fascinating. I read *House Made of Dawn* twice, not because I didn't understand it the first time, but because it resonated with me, and I was compelled to reread it. I didn't dislike any of the assigned reading if that helps at all?"

A long, low whistle emanated from the professor, who cocked an eyebrow at him, clearly impressed at all the reading Sabre had already done in just the first five weeks of the semester.

"It does, though there was no reason to finish the course load in a few weeks' time; wouldn't want you to burn yourself out."

"It was easy, though. I always work ahead. My work-study job is in the library, shelving books and working at the research center desk, answering phone calls and emails. I usually have a ton of downtime and write most of my papers there. Plus, I'm carrying a light course load, four classes, since that's all I need for graduation."

"Well then, let me see what I can do to find you something."

Rummaging around on his desk, Professor Locklear began moving neat stacks of paper until he finally found something of interest. Sabre watched as he perused the list before finally holding it out for him to take.

"Try these; it's the reading list for my Native Literature 103 class, since I'm pretty sure between your papers and what you just told me, you've read most of the books for the 102. See if any of these interest you, and if you have any questions or would care to discuss them, please feel free to come back, or you can stop in my Native Lit discussion group. We meet in the atrium every Wednesday night at eight. Who knows? Perhaps you'll be inspired to participate."

"Thanks, I'll umm... I'll think about it," Sabre said, still staring at the proffered paper. Reaching it meant he'd have to move closer, into the brighter lights above Professor Locklear's desk. Biting his lip, Sabre took the three steps to the desk hesitantly, keeping his eyes on the paper and not the man.

"Are you okay? Is something wrong?"

The concern in his voice was what made Sabre raise his head, and the moment he realized what he'd done, he ducked it again, took the paper, and backed away until he felt the door at his back. Twisting around, he fumbled for the doorknob.

"Wait."

Pausing, Sabre gripped the knob, never turning back.

"If you're hiding in the shadows because of that scar, please know it isn't necessary."

Sabre touched his cheek, stroking his fingertips along the rough edges of the raised, puckered skin as the memory of moonlight striking glass from a busted bottle flashed through his mind. Almost instantly, his breathing picked up, and his chest felt tight as the first stirrings of panic surged through him.

"I've got to go," Sabre muttered, nearly smacking himself in the face with the door as he wrenched it open. "Thanks, professor."

"You're welcome, but..."

Sabre took off before he heard the rest, sprinting up the curry-scented hall, the stench making him gag. Bursting through the outer door, the fall air hit him like a gut punch, carrying with it the scent of dying leaves. He gagged, bile rising in his throat. Skidding to a halt beside a bush, he vomited, grateful nothing but acid remained in his stomach. By the time he finished, he'd broken out in a cold sweat and felt gross and tired, wanting nothing more than to get back to his dorm room and take a long, hot, shower and climb into bed with a movie.

Glancing at the slightly crumpled list he gripped in his fist, Sabre sighed before smoothing it against his thigh, folding it carefully, and tucking it into the pocket of his hoodie. Shoulders slumped, he turned and trudged back toward his dorm, grateful the day was at an end. All in all, it had been both a success and a disaster. Next time, he'd just email his request, he decided, as a cold wind made him shiver and debate what the hell he'd been thinking, going to see his professor in person.

"Stupid," he muttered as his short walk came to an end at his dorm.

For a so-called genius, he sure could be an idiot sometimes.

Chapter 2

GROANING, DRAX TOED off his shoes and slid the elastic from his hair, giving it a quick shake and immediately feeling the tightness at the back of his neck lessening. He'd been fighting a low-grade tension headache all day, and at this point, he was either going to have to bite the bullet and wear it loose or get it cut again. Maybe he'd just have them take a few inches off, nothing as drastic as the undercut he'd gotten the last time. He'd hated it less than a week afterward, and it took forever to grow out. Never again, he told himself once it had. While he couldn't stand to have his hair past his shoulders, he hated it short-short too. No, a happy medium was what was called for, and this time he'd be certain to make his wishes quite clear before anyone started cutting.

The scent of lime, onions, and spices wafted up from the takeout carton at the corner of his desk, and he reached for it, rummaging around in his top drawer for a plastic fork so he might delve into the succulent fried calamari and rice while still hot. An obscene moan rumbled up from his chest the moment the first bite hit his tongue. Licking his lips, he tasted the remnants of roasted pepper, shallots, ginger, and garlic lingering there. So, so good. Taking his time, he savored each bite as he unpacked his briefcase and organized the papers he needed to grade into neat stacks.

By the time he finished his meal, he had his grade book open and ready, two red pens poised to be abused, and a neon yellow highlighter sitting beside them for things he really wished to draw their attention to. Dumping his empty carton in the trash, he stood and stretched, feeling the vertebrae in his back pop in a long line, reminding him he really needed to follow his physician's advice to take regular breaks after sitting at his desk for too long. Maybe he needed to set an alarm or, better still, download an app and establish some intervals for stretching and changing positions he couldn't ignore, though getting up to walk around always seemed silly when there was work to be done. Perhaps he needed to find an activity outside the office—use the gym and pool areas before he found himself making another visit to the chiropractor to have his spine readjusted and aligned. Turning his head, he pushed beneath his chin, enough to get his neck to pop on each side before he ambled into his bedroom and changed into sweatpants and a T-shirt so worn most of the image had faded away.

A quick glance in the mirror made him pause. His reflection showed a man in his twenties, and early twenties at that. He'd lost sight of how many times he was mistaken for a student, and yet, he felt every inch of his thirty-six years, and then some, depending on the day. He really did need to make time for physical activity. Genetics blessed him with a high metabolism, but he feared all the takeout meals he consumed might catch up to him someday. Tomorrow, he vowed as he returned to his chair and picked up the first paper. Tomorrow he'd fit in an hour workout, perhaps in the pool. It had been a long time since he'd swum laps. Once, it used to be the only way to clear his head, the glassy surface of the water shimmering as his body cut through, each rhythm leaving him more settled and at ease.

Drax glanced at the name on the paper and groaned. He hadn't a clue why Carson West was in his Intro to Native Lit class unless, like so many others before him, he'd assumed it would be a gimmie grade. His attendance was spotty at best, one of several students who were making him reconsider his lack of an attendance policy, and when he was in class, he rarely participated. To top it off, his papers always read like they'd been cobbled together at the last minute, regurgitating the basic plot of the story without ever digging beneath the surface to find hidden meanings or draw comparisons to other manuscripts.

Such a vast difference from Sabre's work.

Smiling fondly, he recalled how thrilled and shocked he'd been the first time he encountered one of Sabre's papers. Of course, the moment that initial shock wore off, he'd run it through the plagiarism checker, expecting it to come back at some extremely high percentage that would necessitate a meeting with the student or at the very least, a failing grade. At minimum, he'd expected to issue a warning to be more cautious in the future lest he be forced to bring Sabre up on charges of academic misconduct. Instead, it came back at three percent—and that only for the quotes Sabre had used in highlighting his argument.

What's more, Drax carefully went over Sabre's sources, rereading them to get a better understanding of Sabre's reasoning, much as he explained to the young man earlier in the day. In truth, he wanted to sit with him to discuss some of his reasoning at length and was just about to offer him a seat, again, when he bolted.

Tapping his fingers on the smooth surface of his desk, his thoughts drifted back to that wickedly curved scar that appeared to start at Sabre's hairline, run through his left eyebrow, then curve in an arc toward his cheek, ending at his jawline. What manner of misfortune had befallen him, Drax wondered, pondering whether it was accidental or if someone deliberately marked him that way. He didn't look like the reformed troublemakers who occasionally graced the lecture halls. Of course, he could be wrong, profiling based on appearances and attitude, but the idea of Sabre as a disciplinary problem didn't jive with his work or the vibe Drax got from him.

Loner was more like it. Bookworm. The kind of kid who was book smart, highly intelligent, but lacked social skills or the ability to translate what he read into practical applications. In other words, someone who'd fit right into the world of academia. He wondered what Sabre's plans were after he graduated, all while wishing he had more students like him. It made teaching a far more pleasant experience when the students were engaged and eager to actively participate in discussions about the material. Some days he preached to a room full of cardboard cutouts, propped up by the seats, their eyes held open by an excess of sugar and energy drinks.

With a resigned sigh, he dialed back his melancholy and curiosity about Sabre in order to focus on the paper in front of him.

Big mistake

The first line of Carson's paper spoke of everything that was wrong with him as a student.

The themes of Sherman Alexie's novels include being an Indian part-time, playing blues in a reservation band, running from the devil, rock and roll dreams, nightmares about ancestors, survival, timeless tribes, learning to be a cartoonist, suffering through medical problems, attending an all-white school, and Indian mascots.

Not only did it read like a laundry list, but…scowling, Drax reached for his copies of the assigned material and flipped them over, skimming the back to see that all Carson had done was paraphrase certain ideas from the back of each of the books and make clever references to the titles. At no point, whatsoever, did he reference the actual thread of themes that ran through each story. In fact, Drax wasn't even sure Carson had actually read the books.

Reading line by line, his red pen etched a bloody trail of red ink through the entire paragraph before he left a scathing note beside the mess for Carson to, more than likely, ignore.

It was exhausting.

In the end, he scored a sixty-two—a *D*—and just barely at that. All that had kept the grade from being a failure was the fact that Carson managed to vaguely discuss common plots between the two novels, a sign he'd read something, though if Drax were to venture a guess, it would be that Carson looked online for summaries or someone else's writing on the subject.

Shaking his head, he entered the score in his gradebook and moved on to the next paper, soft blues on the radio, the whine of a sad guitar harmonizing with his mood. It was going to be a long night indeed. Another in a long stream of evenings spent hunched over the desk, shoulder's aching. As he plodded along, he was reminded of the joy he got from teaching, the instances when something clicked for a student, and he actually saw the moment of clarity in their eyes. Literature, for him, had always been about the ability to step outside the real world and go somewhere else, another time, another place, another state of being. He cherished the opportunity to be introduced to new ideas, thoughts, feelings, and experiences of people who'd grown up profoundly different from the way he had. Teaching others to view literary works the same way was always his goal, and the one thing he needed to remember was for every Carson West, there was a Sabre Lord, and those were the ones he was meant to reach.

Chapter 3

FANNING HIMSELF, SABRE opened the freezer door and sighed in relief as the cold air wafted against his cheeks. His skin prickled with pulses of energy, static along his flesh. Restless and itchy, sometimes painful, still, he sought to bury it, stave off the jolts of pure need shooting through him. He wouldn't be able to ignore the craving for much longer; already he'd pushed himself to his limits through sheer stubbornness and exhaustion, but the compulsion was getting heavier, like a tight, wet band around his throat, choking off reason.

His stomach lurched, still upset from earlier. The thought of eating made him wrinkle his nose, but he knew if he didn't, if he kept skipping meals and eating junk, he'd be too weak and worn out to do much once he was finally forced to give in to his body's yearning. Scrubbing a hand over his face, he groaned and reached for a steak, plucking it from a pile of meat before slamming the freezer door. Tossing it in the microwave, he hit the auto-defrost button, set it for eight minutes, and busied himself poking around in the fridge to hunt down the rest of his meal.

A wilting head of lettuce, a sad-looking tomato, a slightly wrinkled cucumber, and a crinkled radish were the only things in the crisper. Not wanting to waste them, he pulled the vegetables out and set about dicing them up, reminded at the last minute he should probably add a boiled egg for more protein. Protein would be essential in the upcoming week.

Before long he was sitting down to his meal, hesitantly picking at the food. Though unappealing, he forced down every bite, gagging a few times. He did not want to puke again, under any circumstances. He was just glad he'd made it outside in time. His cheeks burned with humiliation over the memory of the way he fled. Professor Lockland probably thought he was high or completely deranged after the way he acted. Absently, his fingertips stroked over the edges of his scar, and he shivered, feeling sick with hate and disgust. He was always so hyperaware of its presence, hating the questioning stares and outright pity or revulsion he'd seen on far too many faces.

Being a good student who rarely needed to go to his teachers for help made it easy for him to blend into the shadows and be forgotten, though sometimes it really sucked. Some of the discussions that took place around him made him long to jump in. He scribbled ideas in his notebook as he listened, thoughts inspired by the other students' words and the teachers' discourse. It was really what had drawn him to Professor Lockland's office. Well, that and the fact the reading material fascinated him, and he craved more.

Touching his face again, he traced his scar, loathing it and all the things it prohibited him from feeling comfortable taking part in. When it first happened, he didn't try to hide, believing the old adage of "chicks dig scars," only he'd never had much of an interest in chicks. With guys, he figured it would be easier somehow, a kinship of shared recklessness, accidents, and misspent youth, though his was caused by none of those things.

In a way, that was as big an issue as its existence—the fact he hadn't gotten it by any of the usual means. The scar was a badge of honor that shouldn't have happened, and while it came with a tale, he didn't care to share.

If you're hiding in the shadows because of that scar, please know it isn't necessary.

Only Professor Locklear was wrong, because he'd come to hate the questions he was asked once people saw it. Like *did it hurt?* Well, no shit, it hurt. What the fuck did they think? That it appeared there—puckered and healed without him noticing until he looked in the mirror? Yet for all the shitty questions, the one question he hated the most was "What happened?" because those words always triggered the memory of confrontation and fear and hurled him headlong into a panic attack. Hell, this afternoon it hadn't even taken a question, simply the act of revealing himself to someone new had ramped up his anxiety to the point of almost unbearable. Spots danced before his eyes, the room tilted, and all that kept him off the floor was his tenuous hold on the door and sheer stubborn will.

So much for his anxiety meds, which reminded him...

Shoving his chair backward, he got up from the table and crossed the room to the fridge, fetching his meds from the top. For the hundredth time that semester, he was grateful for having a single. The headache that came from all of the begging he'd had to do to the student housing director was well worth the effort. In the end, his grades and his goals were what tipped the scales in his favor, putting him above some of the other students who'd submitted a similar request.

Grumbling bitterly about how the pill still barely made a dent in his stress and anxiety levels, even after the newest adjustment, he swallowed it dry, grimacing at the bitter taste. On the chalkboard beside the stove, he wrote juice, drink mix, and coffee. He could drink water, but he hated the mineral taste of what came from the tap, and he'd forgotten to pick up a jug of distilled again.

He made short work of the dishes, wiped down the counter and stove, turned out the lights, and headed out into the combination library, sitting room, living room, study space, and den—the cramped room filled with bookcase shelves, his desk, one worn, faded, overstuffed easy chair with duct tape across the seat, and the entertainment center that took up the far wall, movies piled around his flat screen TV.

This space looked lived in, with poetry and prose in little slips of notepaper stuck to corkboards all over the walls, so unlike the starkness of his bedroom. Someone had told him once he shouldn't take his work into his sleeping space, nor should he keep his television or computer there because the distraction would keep him from a good night's sleep. Someone else had included music and went so far as to suggest a notepad wouldn't be a good idea either, and they were right. More often than not, he woke around four a.m., groggy and groping for a notebook and a pen, fingers brushing against the lamp cord as he sought to turn it on. The one concession he'd refused to make was to leave that notebook in the living room.

What it meant, however, was that his bedroom contained only his bed, an end table, a lamp and the clothing in his closet. His bedroom was a place to sleep and nothing more. He tended to spend the majority of his time in his study space, grateful that this dorm wasn't filled with party people. Tonight, he sank into the chair and reached for the remote, turning on the TV and flipping channels until he found an old show he'd grown up watching.

It would do.

He left the unread books on the end table beside the chair, ignoring the computer on his desk and the half-finished papers waiting for him. They weren't due for a while anyway. Turning off the lights, he kicked back in his chair, closed his eyes and listened to the sounds of the show. Audience laughter and a grumpy old man threatening to throw everyone off his property.

Nostalgia washed over him, a calming, amusing warmth; almost perfect, only...there was no one to share it with. In all likelihood that was the other reason he stopped by Professor Locklear's office. Some hope he refused to acknowledge, some need for his simple request to turn into full-fledged conversation.

And yet, as soon as he offered, you fled, ya idiot.

Berating himself came easily. He constantly battled depression and the loneliness of his existence, going back and forth between treasuring his solitude and anonymity and longing for human connection. If only it were as easy as the jovial camaraderie and laid back interactions he saw on TV. It always seemed effortless for others. He watched them in the corridors, in the dining hall and rec room, on the quad and in the athletic center, even off campus and around town, engaging in easy laughter and conversation in a way he'd never felt comfortable taking part in, even before the damage done to his face.

Because they can't laugh at you; they can't ask questions you'd rather not answer or give you looks of pity when they learn about your past, his damned inner voice spoke loudly to remind him. Spouting truth from a pit of self-deprecationn. Watching from a distance meant never having to put himself out there. From them, he derived the basis for his characters, studied dialogue and interactions until he could replicate them on the page. His fiction benefited from his observations, but make-believe was little comfort on a night like this.

He'd prefer the distraction of conversation to the thoughts filling his head, but that was the trouble with trying so hard to exist in the shadows. Sometimes, the darkness got to be too much.

Chapter 4

THE SCENT OF ONIONS and sizzling meat permeated the little diner. For all his attempts at curbing his takeout habit, Drax found himself once again standing in line to place an order for a patty-melt basket, intent on heading back to his office and getting some research done. He got a coffee, too—large, black, and piping hot the way he liked it, knowing he needed to cut down on that, too, but at least he'd learned to take it without sugar. Still, his progress reflected the effort invested. He'd managed to work in an hour and a half swim, and though his shoulders were sore from the endeavor, it felt good to slip into the water and let his thoughts melt away in a haze of movement.

A familiar hoodie caught his eye moments before his butt connected with the seat he'd planned to wait in. Since that day in his office, he'd tried to find a moment to speak to Sabre, but the young man always seemed to slip through the door right before the lecture was scheduled to start and slip out again as soon as he finished speaking. Funny, but he couldn't recall Sabre engaging in similar behavior before. In fact, he was certain Sabre had always been one of the first in the classroom, scribbling furiously in a notebook while the rest of the students filed in.

That meant he'd deliberately altered his schedule to avoid talking to him. Well, that just wouldn't do.

Passing a row of booths, Drax approached the young man, who was eating with one hand and writing with the other. For a moment, Drax paused, admiring the neatness of his penmanship and the sheer skill of managing both simultaneously without seeming to miss a beat. Just when he was about to comment, his eyes landed on the book tower at the edge of the table, and his jaw dropped at the top two titles.

"Where in the world did you find that?"

Sabre jerked, startled, pen dropping onto the notepad as he raised his head.

"Sorry, I didn't mean to spook you. I haven't seen another copy of this in years," Drax remarked as he lifted *The Ghost Dance Religion and Wounded Knee* and turned it over in his hands. Sabre ducked his head, tugging at his hood as Drax slid into the booth across from him.

"Hey. I was serious when I said you don't need to hide your face from me. You don't need to dash out of class as soon as the lecture is over, and you don't need to slip in at the last minute either. I don't know why you felt the need to run the other day, but I hope it wasn't because of anything I said or did."

Sabre shook his head, and Drax waited patiently to see if he'd say anything.

"No," Sabre remarked at last, his voice soft and a little bit muffled. "I'm really shy and nervous about someone seeing it for the first time, so once I realized you had, I started to feel overwhelmed."

"So we're good now?"

"Yes, sir."

"Marvelous, then how about you tell me where you found this?"

Lifting his head a little, Sabre actually met Drax's eyes across the table. Drax was quick to give him a smile, hoping to encourage him not to hide anymore.

"Eclipse Books on Seventh. In fact, I found a considerable number of interesting books there and cleaned off half the shelf." Sabre remarked. Reaching for the backpack beside him, Sabre lifted out several publications, spreading them on the table for Drax to peruse, the sight drawing a whistle from him as he took in the titles.

"This is quite impressive. Some of these have been out of print for a while. I have upper-level students who haven't been able to find copies, including through online sources."

"The owner said they'd been languishing in bookcases gathering dust. In fact, he cussed some of those same online sellers you were referring to. Said they make people lazy and keep them from being able to appreciate the process of browsing shelves and spending hours among the stacks. I admit I tend to agree. I'd rather go to a bookstore and search for something than be able to type in a title and have it instantly pop up. Where's the fun in that? Half the fun of browsing is finding a handful of other books you weren't searching for but would love to read anyway."

"I also happen to agree. That being said, I should be ashamed of myself. I forgot Eclipse was there. I guess I just assumed it had vanished like so many others and never bothered to look. Thank you for reminding me."

When Sabre rewarded him with a small smile, Drax grinned in return.

"You're welcome," Sabre said. "I go there all the time."

Pausing, Drax lay the book on the table and regarded Sabre intently. "Do you mind if I ask you a question?"

"No."

"All right then, why did you take my class if it wasn't a requirement?"

Sabre shrugged and fiddled with the hoodie's ties. "I wanted a literature class, and when I started looking at the book lists for other classes, I kept coming across books I'd already read. I didn't want to rehash old material. I wanted to learn something new. That's what college is supposed to be about, right?"

"It is, but you'd be surprised at how few students look at it from that perspective. Many are merely looking to do their time, scrape by, and head out into the working world where, unfortunately, they then look for ways to barely scrape by at their jobs. It's sad, to see the waste of so much potential."

"Then why even come to college? To me, it's such a waste to not get as much out of the experience as I possibly can. Browsing the reading list for your class, what jumped out at me was that I'd never even heard of any of the books on it. An author should be well read, and that's what I aspire to be. When the opportunity presented itself, I had to jump on it, and I'm glad I did. Everything I've been exposed to so far has been fascinating. I'm actually learning something, rather than just going through the motions to get a grade."

"I'm glad to hear that. I have to admit, you made my day when you came to my office to ask for extra reading. The fact that you've gone above and beyond that really blows me away."

Shrugging, Sabre glanced away shyly. "I like to read."

"There's liking to read, and then there is a genuine thirst for knowledge. You strike me as the type who has a passion for learning. If I were to venture a guess, I'd say you grew up around books; your folks read to you when you were little and bought you a ton of novels as you were growing up."

"I wish. My folks died in an apartment fire when I was three. I went into the system. Books became my friends from the time I learned how to read. I didn't want to be underfoot or cause trouble. I witnessed what happened to the kids who did that. Some places were really good, but others? You could do absolutely nothing wrong and still draw someone's ire."

Drax blinked, completely shocked at just how off-base his assessment had been. "I...I'm sorry you had to experience something like that."

Sabre shrugged again and slipped the end of a tie in his mouth, chewing on it for a moment before catching himself and tugging it free. "It could have been worse. I was lucky. More homes were good than bad, and a few were truly special. My last foster family was the one to make sure I was able to tour schools, get applications, letters of recommendation, financial aid, application fee wavers, and all of that. I can't thank them enough for making sure I had a shot at the future I wanted and wasn't going to be forced to settle because of my circumstances."

"That was admirable of them. I'm glad you have people who care about you."

"Yeah, it was. I'll always be grateful to them for that. I've been saving money from my afterschool job since I was old enough to work, but I knew it would never be enough. I guess it was sort of a pipe dream I refused to give up on."

Drax nodded, those words hitting close to home. It reminded him of his mother's story of growing up in a big family and fearing she'd have to sacrifice her education to work and help with her siblings. A full scholarship had saved her from that fate, but it could have easily turned out differently. "And it's a good thing too. Look how far it's gotten you. A few more months and you'll be a college graduate. What are your plans?"

"Finish up my novel over the winter break while preparing to enter the master's program for creative writing once school starts back up again."

"Here?"

"Yeah, I couldn't imagine going anywhere else. This place is home. I know I can't stay on campus forever, though. Eventually, I'll have to look for something in town, but I've never felt more at home than in these mountains."

Chuckling, Drax nodded his thanks to the waitress who brought over the bag containing his food. His interest wasn't on takeout at the moment, though, but on the conversation he was enjoying. "I know the feeling."

"Did you grow up in this town?" Sabre asked.

"No, but much like you, I fell in love with it while attending college here. Then I stayed for grad school, and by the time I finished, I decided I wanted to teach at the school and work on my doctorate."

"How's that coming?"

"Slowly, even sluggishly at times, but I'll get there. Sometimes I feel like I'm drowning in notes and new material."

Chuckling at that, Sabre gave a quick glance at his own work. "Do you ever take a break to do something fun?"

"Not as often as I should. Even when I do take a break from the books, I typically end up doing field research or working with a group on grant writing or setting up programs, volunteering, that sort of thing. How about you? Surely you've experienced some of the more clandestine college traditions like keg parties and screaming out the dorm windows to relieve stress during exam week."

Wrinkling his nose, Sabre blew the strand of hair over his eyes, making it flutter. "Not really. I mean, I kind of ended up in the middle of a dorm party once, and someone puked on my shoes. Not pleasant. Not my scene. Too loud, too many people talking and yelling over one another and the music. I ended up heading to the library to read in peace. Invested in a good pair of noise-canceling headphones, too, after enduring the first scream night. I didn't see the point then, still don't, how the hell is someone supposed to study with all that noise going on?"

"There is more to life than reading, you know—not that there is anything wrong with getting wrapped up in a good book, but you have to have more interests than that."

Sabre shrugged and scratched the back of his neck. "I like music, especially paired with a good book. I like films too. I try to make a bowl of popcorn and watch movies at least once a week without being distracted by assignments and stuff. I absolutely adore horror flicks. Autumn is my favorite season. I love the way everything looks, smells—the whole aesthetic is just phenomenal. Every fall I make caramel corn instead of plain buttered, so I have a treat during October and November. I do a countdown to Halloween with a movie each day for the week leading up to it. It's a great way to de-stress."

Tapping his fingers on the table, Sabre chewed on his lower lip while Drax waited for him to continue. "I love going to open mic nights. I try not to miss them unless I'm overwhelmed with schoolwork. I really enjoy going to the movies in the park when they have something interesting. I love when the campus library or even the one in town has a reading scheduled. Some of those have been truly inspiring. I'm also part of two writers groups and a book club that meets every Thursday night at the town library. I know, I know, more reading, but the book of the week is a nice break from classroom stuff, and our discussions are riveting."

"I would think so, considering it's a chance to infuse a bit of fiction into your week."

"That's pretty much why I do it; for the escapism and immersion into a world where anything is possible."

"So what are you reading right now?"

"*Night Without Stars*. So far, it's a pretty interesting read."

"That's always helpful. Tell me something— Have you ever attended a story circle?"

"You mean the kind where everyone brings a piece of flash fiction or a two-to-three-page short story to read and get feedback on?"

"Something like that, only without the feedback. In this case, I'm talking about the kind where stories of the past are retold among personal stories and stories that people have picked up in their travels. Some contain life lessons, some the history of a family. Some even recount real, though embellished events, from time to time. Some stories are purely for entertainment purposes, though often based on a real misfortune or unfortunate event. There's one coming up on Saturday. I'm taking a van load of my advanced Native Lit students up to listen. You're welcome to join us."

Sabre's eyes widened a bit as the tip of his tongue poked out to lick his lip. Drax watched him open his mouth and close it, like he was measuring his words and trying not to appear too eager. "Are you sure? If it's for your advanced students, I'm not sure I'd be able to keep up."

"You'll do just fine; all you need is a sharp mind and to be a good listener, both of which are characteristics you already possess."

A slow smile brightened Sabre's features. "Then I'd love to go as long as you're sure there's room."

"There's room; we always have one or two empty seats, so if you'd like to claim one, just be outside the library on Saturday morning at seven. It's a bit of a drive."

"Okay, I'll be there."

"Good deal. I'll see you then. I think you'll get a lot out of it."

"Thanks!" Flashing him a smile, Sabre began gathering up his things. "I'd better get moving. I've got my Art of the Motion Picture class starting in about ten minutes. We'll be discussing our analysis of *Bonnie and Clyde*, especially the dramatics of the chase sequence and shootout."

"Color or black and white?"

"Black and white."

"That's the best version, there's always something a bit gritty and raw about watching in black and white instead of color."

"That's because color can make things look hokey or detract from the emotion of a piece, especially when filmmakers try to get cute and weave symbolism where it isn't needed."

Amen to that, Drax thought to himself. "Unfortunately, we live in an era where bright flashing colors, loud vivid explosions, and tons of skin are needed to capture and keep people's attention. It's a shame. I think sometimes the storytelling gets lost among all the bells and whistles."

"Don't get me started on that, or I'll never get to class. Speaking of which, I've really got to go. As it is, I'll have to run all the way there just to make it on time, but it was great talking to you. I hope we can do it again soon."

He took off, ties on the hoodie flapping as he raced out the door. As soon as he disappeared from sight, Drax smacked himself on the forehead and dragged his hand down, scrubbing it over his face a few times. What the hell had he been thinking, inviting Sabre along to the story circle? Though at least *that* invitation had come out, instead of the first one to flash through his mind. Shaking his head, he checked the time, grateful for the additional free hour before his last block of classes. His stomach rumbled, and since he was already sitting in the booth, he decided to eat his food before it got cold. Still, how close he'd come to asking a student on a date, simply because the conversation had been enjoyable, continued to run through his mind.

"I really need to get a grip," he muttered, stirring his now cold coffee. "And a date with someone my own age or barring that, not in one of my classes."

He chugged what was left of the cold brew, grimacing at the bitter aftertaste before digging into his food, one thought running over and over through his mind. Sabre might be his student now...but soon enough, the semester would end.

Chapter 5

SITTING IN THE BACK of the van, staring out the window, Sabre watched the trees swaying as they passed. Breezy and slightly chilly, the weather was about average for fall. The mountains looked beautiful, with clumps of reds, oranges, and golds dotted here and there, mixed with the vivid hues of evergreens. They'd stand out more come winter, proudly poking up through the snow. An image flashed through his mind of hot cocoa with tiny marshmallows and sledding down bumpy slopes at exhilarating speeds. Smiling at the memory, he looked forward to the thrill of rocketing downhill and those moments of perfect peace he experienced alone in the wilderness, though there were times when it was lonely, having no one to share an afternoon of ice fishing with.

Sighing, he closed his eyes, attempting to block out the conversations of the other students going on around him; letting his mind drift toward pleasant memories and plans for the future. He'd agonized over the decision to come, wanting to experience the story circle, but terrified at the thought of meeting so many new people all at once. In the end, he'd discussed it with his doctor, explaining about the panic attack the previous week and how anxious he'd been lately, and they'd both agreed the current dose wasn't working, so he upped it again. He was moving farther and farther away from leaving those meds in the past. He hated being dependent on anything, let alone a pill, but the reality was he didn't function well without it, which sucked.

The slight dip in the seat as someone dropped down beside him startled him from his thoughts, and blinking, he glanced over to see a large form occupying what was once empty space.

"Hey, I just thought I'd introduce myself. My name's Benjamin Thunder Hawk Matthews. I'm in professor Locklear's Advanced Survey of Native Literature class and his Native Lit discussion group; in fact, most of us are. You'll have to forgive us for being rude; we can be a rowdy bunch when we get together, but that's no excuse for not introducing ourselves. Are you new to the program?"

Heart hammering in his chest, Sabre swallowed hard and licked his lips. "Nope, I'm a senior. I'm in Intro to Native Literature."

"Whoa... And yet you're here on the way to a story circle."

Tensing, Sabre shot a sidelong glance at Ben, peering past the edge of his hoodie. "Yeah...so?"

"Just...you ever been to one before?"

"Nope."

"Bucking for extra credit or something?"

Sabre had to chuckle at that. It would figure Ben would think that was the reason. Why couldn't people just do something because they were interested and wanted to learn? "No, I was just curious. I'm a creative writing major, figured it would be a new experience. Who knows? It's feasible that one day I'll end up writing it into a book or something."

"Make sure you include me—that's Thunder Hawk, two words, not one all squished together like most folks tend to write it. So, if you're here for the experience, why hide all the way in back?"

"Not particularly social."

"I can respect that."

At that point, Sabre figured Ben would go back to wherever it was he'd been sitting; instead, he lingered as the van bounced over a rutted section of road.

"So, what can we call you, since 'Not Particularly Social' would get pretty tiresome after a while, and I'm reasonably sure it counts as a title, or at minimum, an occupation rather than an actual name."

Sabre snorted, then broke into a full belly laugh, leaning over until his head touched the back of the seat in front of him. As unexpected as it had been, he welcomed the laugh, despite the sudden unease and apprehension of dealing with a stranger. Finally, he raised his head, a small smile still stretching his lips.

"I'm Sabre."

"Nice to meet you. It's always good to have someone new take an interest in these trips. It doesn't happen often enough."

"Exactly how many students are in the Native Studies program?"

"Native Studies is the other van, totally different major, but there's about thirty-two or so; it fluctuates. They were as high as forty-five at one point and at their lowest, as far as I know, anyway, they were down to eighteen. For Native Lit majors, there's twenty-seven of us. Needless to say, Professor Locklear is our advisor and teaches most of the classes."

"How big is the department?"

"Just three professors, but only Professor Locklear and the Native Studies teacher, Professor Begay, are full time. The third professor, Grace Windtalker, only teaches a few of the advanced classes. She's getting up there in years, but man, the things she's experienced firsthand make for the best lessons and discussions. I always make sure to sit in when she gives a lecture or heads a panel at a conference. She comes at things from a perspective that not many can speak from. You'll see. She's one of the storytellers tonight."

"So what kind of stories should we expect? True stories, or are there old myths and legends or just stories someone made up?"

"All three. You'll see. It's impossible to describe, but once you've gone through it, you'll understand. Just don't expect it to be like anything you've ever experienced."

Sabre smiled a little and lifted his head, biting his lip as he turned toward Ben. He was a big guy, towering over Sabre, even seated. The brown-and-tan flannel he wore looked soft and warm, and the grin he gave Sabre eased the knot that had begun to form in the pit of his stomach at the start of the conversation. "Sounds like I'm in for a good time."

"I promise you this, you won't be bored. It's conceivable you'll even find you're not as anti-social as you think."

Sabre snorted, glancing away again. "Somehow I doubt that."

"We'll see."

Lapsing into silence for a bit, Sabre found himself lulled by the pull of drifting daydreams. Ben would make a comment or ask a question, and yet, never once was Sabre annoyed as he usually was. Instead, he responded in kind, reluctantly at first, but pretty soon the silence between them grew shorter and shorter until the only gaps were pauses for thought or breath. When the van finally pulled to a jerky halt, Sabre looked around, stunned at the quaint little town outside the window.

Columns of brick buildings lined what could only be the town's Main Street, with houses stretching back in tidy rows. Children played on well-kept lawns with dogs nipping at their heels or running in pursuit of tennis balls. A large totem sat several feet from where they'd parked, several smaller ones surrounding it, and in the distance, Sabre could see smoke rising from a bonfire in the center of a vast field of clover. Several folks were already gathered around, sitting in cloth folding chairs in a wide variety of colors, much like the blankets many of them had tucked across their laps.

The breeze carried with it the scent of pancakes, sausage, eggs, and bacon sizzling on a griddle beside a pot of bubbling oatmeal. Just the scent of it made his stomach rumble. Three men were setting up a table, coolers at their feet.

"Did I forget to mention they feed us too? Three meals, all home-cooked. Mmm mmm, am I looking forward to that. Food court meals get tiring after a while."

"Tell me about it. So um, what do those represent? Sabre asked as he gestured toward the totems.

"The families who make up the village. Some are really old, and some are newer. Whenever a new family moves out here, they add their totem. They never take any away, though, even when the last member of a family passes on. It stands as a remembrance that they were here."

"Why is that one taller than all of the others?"

"It's symbolic of the tribe as a whole rather than any one individual branch of it. Hey, words of advice for the day. Put aside a great deal of what history books and Hollywood movies have filled your head with. Most of that crap is sensationalist bullshit. Folks who have never taken the time to learn the truth or live it appropriate pieces of our culture and history and slap it all together in a hodge-podge mess. They don't give two shits about accuracy; it's all about perpetuating the same stereotypes over and over."

Sabre nodded, recalling a debate back in high school over whether or not history was subjective, given that the victors could put whatever spin on it they wanted. "I'm not big on stereotypes, and I hate clichés so no worries."

"Good deal."

Sabre waited for Ben to vacate the seat, and then he followed, stepping from the van and feeling a soft mist carried along on the breeze. Inhaling deeply, he let the fresh scent settle into his lungs, grateful for professor Locklear's warning about the dampness in the air. Dressed in a long-sleeved T-shirt beneath his hoodie he'd stashed gloves in the pouch, just in case. Shoving his hands in his pockets, he ducked his head and trudged along behind Ben. There were scant few blooms left in the meadow, and what remained was weathered and burned, a few browned peddles clinging here and there, the seed caps long since disbursed. Rich, clean scents surrounded him: grass and soil, sunshine and the minty tang of peppermint. Inhaling deeply, he committed the scents to memory, knowing he'd want to describe it in a story one day.

"I see you've met Benjamin."

Professor Locklear's voice startled him from his creative contemplation, the first stirrings of a scene already beginning to develop in his mind. Returning his focus to the present, he glanced over to see the older man watching him.

"Ummm, Ben... Yeah, he seems like a really nice guy."

"He is. He's come out to quite a few of these with me over the years. He'll be finishing up his bachelor's in the spring the same as you, and then, unfortunately, he's heading up the coast to Washington for his master's. Wish we still had a program like that here."

"What happened to it?"

"Not enough interest. To be honest, we're barely holding on to our undergraduate programs. They struggle to get funding each year."

"That sucks; the program of studies offers something different not a lot of colleges include. I'd have been stuck taking a Hemmingway class this semester if it wasn't for your course, which would have been boring as hell since I read all of his stuff back in high school."

"Must have been a really affluent school then. Most public schools did away with the classics years ago."

"Unfortunately, mine fell into that category. I read his work for a term paper freshman year. I wanted to focus on an author who wasn't on our reading list, which didn't make my teacher real thrilled."

"Really? I'd have thought you'd be praised for going above and beyond what the curriculum offered."

"I imagine if it had been someone like you, I would have been, but she was pissed 'cause I generated a ton more work for her. She spent time fact checking what I'd done since she hadn't read him."

Drax snorted and shot Sabre a look that was difficult to interpret. "That hardly seems fair. Out of curiosity, what did you score on the paper?"

"An *A*, but there was a note attached, basically demanding I stick with the assigned materials for the duration of her class."

"And did you?"

"Nope," Sabre remarked, popping the *p*, laughing, and pleased when Professor Locklear started laughing too.

"I doubt I would have either. Sometimes, it's better to ask forgiveness than permission, and other times, it's just better to say to hell with it, and do what works for you."

"Exactly."

"Come on, let's grab some grub and some spiced cider. If you want a good seat close to the fire, you'd better stake it out now. Once things start filling up, you'll find yourself in no-man's-land."

"Somehow, I think that might be a better spot for me."

"Oh no, not today. Trust me when I say you want to be up-front for the full experience. I promise you, no one will care about your scar; it won't even be the worse one out here today."

Sighing, Sabre rubbed the back of his neck, hesitant. "Maybe," he conceded at last, following Professor Locklear to get food.

Chapter 6

DRAX STARED ACROSS the circle, watching the flickers of firelight play across Sabre's face. As soon as the sunset, he'd pushed back his hoodie, and now Drax could see the black and gold of his hair in the flames. An odd color and yet, it looked random in that way that appeared completely natural; another quirk among many that was beginning to make Sabre stand out.

With rapt attention, Sabre studied Grace as she launched into her story, and even Drax tingled with anticipation at the thought of what she might tell.

"Several generations ago," began Grace. "A baby girl was born into the Lenape tribe and as she grew, she discovered that she possessed the ability to change her form from that of a human to that of a bobcat."

Now this was new. Grace was a collector of old tales, but Drax had never heard her share this one.

"Because the elders of her tribe no longer shared the old stories with the people, she was not aware that her ability was not a thing to be feared. Instead, she hid it from her parents, and her grandparents and even the young man she eventually married. She viewed it as something shameful, something abnormal that she should never do again."

Spellbound, the story circle seemed to breathe collectively, all eyes trained on her as she sat regally, hands folded in her lap, the long ends of her sweater concealing them.

"A time came when the winter ran long and game was exceedingly scarce. The village stores were running low, and the people were growing thin. Hunters roamed far and wide in search of game, only to return empty-handed with weary horses and tired spirits. The snow fell deeply and the chore of trudging through it began to wear on many of them, and they began to despair. In her lodge house, the young woman struggled to make what food they had stretch, but without meat, regaining strength was difficult."

She painted a bleak picture, but Drax knew these stories had a way of turning themselves around and more often than not, teaching a lesson. It would be interesting to see which one she'd chosen to present today.

"When another hunting party returned with nothing, the young woman went to the frozen creek and prayed for guidance. As she prayed, she received a sign from the gods in the form of a fat, white rabbit who'd nosed up out of his burrow. In an instant, she yanked off her clothing and dropped it into the snow, shifted, and killed the bunny, bringing it back to her lodge once she'd returned to her human form and redressed. Of course, there was rejoicing, but one rabbit would only feed her family and her extended family for a day, and after that, they would have nothing again. And what of the other people in the village?"

Drax's gaze once again landed on Sabre and his lips curled in a smile when he saw the wide-eyed, open-mouthed expression on the young man's face and the way his drink seemed frozen, midway to his lips, as if he'd forgotten how to move.

"That night, she devised a plan, and early in the morning as the sun was barely peeking over the horizon, she headed out, using her superior senses to sniff out game. That day, she delivered several fat rabbits and a large turkey to families in the village, discreetly, and continued this practice each day. With their strength renewed, and praise to the spirits for blessing them, the hunters headed out, intent on harvesting bigger game."

Tales of long winters and survival were widespread in their culture, but Drax sensed something different about this tale and in the way Grace seemed to be peering straight at Sabre as she told it. A figment of his imagination, perhaps, but it certainly seemed as if she was telling the story directly to Sabre, whose eyes hadn't left hers since she began.

"Unknown to them, she headed out that day as well, following the scent trail of a herd of deer she'd detected several days before. Locating them, she culled an old one from their midst and herded it directly into the path of the hunters, whose arrows were true. That night, the village feasted, but even as they did, a story began to circulate around the village of a bobcat seen slinking in the shadows beneath the trees. One of the hunters professed to witnessing it running the deer to them."

With sudden clarity, Drax began to understand the point of the tale.

"Many spoke of the spirits walking among them, coming to show favor to their village and help them survive the trials of the long winter. Others spoke of shapeshifters of the past, and the blessings they'd brought to the people. As these nearly forgotten stories were retold, the young woman listened in shock and awe as the people praised the ability and those who had once possessed it, and lamented the fact that there had not been a shape-shifter born among their people for several generations. Hearing this, her heart was filled with joy, because she'd learned that she no longer had anything to fear or be ashamed of. Standing, she came before the tribal fire, with all of the village gathered round, and there before them, showed her second form."

As Drax watched, Sabre sucked in a deep breath, his leg bouncing up and down with what looked to be either anticipation or nervous energy. To watch him be so animated and so enraptured by the story was a thing of beauty. To see him show his face, radiating with joy, filled Drax with pride at having gotten him to come out with them today. Emotions flared, filling his belly with a mix of desire and longing, and he quickly attempted to stamp those feelings out, reminding himself that Sabre was a student—his student. While not unheard of, such things were frowned upon.

"That night, songs were sung and the village danced and celebrated her and all she had done to save them. For the rest of her days, she held a place of honor among her people, and before her passing, she was able to witness the birth of her grandson, who carried the same trait. And because the songs had continued to be sung and the stories continued to be told, he was never forced to suffer a moment of shame or fear at what he was, nor did any of the others born after him."

She smiled as she brought the story to an end, and in the pause that followed, Drax thought about perceptions and how, too often, one judged themselves far more harshly than the world would ever judge them. Sabre clearly hadn't learned that yet. Perhaps he would reflect back on this moment and that story in those instances when he thought to shrink away and hide his face, and realize that there was no reason to hide. Applause erupted, and many surged to their feet, stomping and whistling to show their appreciation for Grace and her brilliant storytelling skills.

Chapter 7

THE CIRCLE BROKE UP not long after Grace was finished speaking. It was easy to see why her tale had been left for last. Who would want to follow that? Sabre shook his head and reached for his hoodie, fingers stilling on the cloth midway through the act of pulling it up over his head. Her story echoed through his mind, and as others headed for the refreshment table, Sabre looked around for Grace. Spotting her long white hair flowing loose as she moved through the crowd, he followed her.

He didn't have to go far. She paused and nimbly climbed onto a large bolder away from the fire's glow, the moonlight shimmering off the granite surface, making her appear almost ethereal. For a moment, he paused to drink in the sight, another memory to add to the collection of memories he'd amassed over the course of the day. His thumb and forefinger itched for the feel of a pen sliding between them as he recorded them all.

"Professor Windtalker, that was an amazing story."

"Thank you, and it's Grace. Out here, there's no need for formalities."

"Do you mind if I join you?"

"Please do."

"Thanks," Sabre remarked before scrambling up onto the rock across from her. "So, was that really a legend of the Lenape tribe, or was it fiction?"

"All fiction is rooted in truth."

"So how much was truth, and how much was made up?"

She quirked an eyebrow at him and cocked her head to the side. "That is a question you'll have to ask yourself. In the end, it all comes down to beliefs.

What do you believe is possible? Do you think a woman could ever turn into a bobcat or any animal for that matter? If the answer is yes, then you should assume the story is real. If the answer is no, then you accept it as fiction."

Sabre opened his mouth, then snapped it shut, studying her for several long moments.

"This world is full of mysteries. Some know this but are willing to deny it in order to fit into what they believe is 'proper' society. Others refuse to believe it, even when the evidence is right in front of their faces, while there are those for whom the mysterious is a normal part of life, and they embrace it," she remarked. "The question is, which are you?"

"A believer," he said, keeping his voice soft and low.

"Then do not hide it, celebrate it," she told him.

He paused a moment, chewing his lower lip before finally deciding to plunge right in with the question he'd truly wished to ask. "So, do you believe a person can turn into an animal?"

Fixing him with a stern look, she nodded. "I don't just believe it, I know it to be fact, and so do you."

His mouth dropped open again, and all he could do was swallow several times as he stumbled over words. "Wh...how... I-I...you... I don't..."

"Please don't insult either of us by attempting to lie. Like calls to like; I sensed what you were the moment Ben introduced us. No doubt he sensed it too."

"B-Ben is..."

"Do you find it so difficult to believe there are others like you?"

"I—yeah actually I do. I've never met anyone else who could shift. Can... Is Professor Locklear a shifter too?"

"Drax is not, no, though he knows of us and what we can do, as do many others who are here today. Trust that this is a safe place for our kind. Now tell me, how is it that no one told you of your heritage and how many varieties of shifters there are?"

Sabre felt his cheeks heat up beneath her scrutiny. Her piercing gaze made him feel as if she were trying to peer into his soul.

"What are you?" he blurted, then slapped a hand over his mouth. "I'm sorry, that was rude of me."

"No, it wasn't. It was honest. I am a silver fox. And in case you're wondering,

Ben is a brown bear. And you are?"

Shrugging, he ducked his head a bit. "A ferret."

"Ahh, well now, that explains the elusiveness, and your extreme focus too. Drax has spoken quite highly of the papers you've submitted in his class, and I must say, after having the opportunity to read your latest piece on the Culture of Death in Native Literature, I'm duly impressed. The hours of research that went into it and the materials utilized went above and beyond what we expect to see in an entry-level class."

"I guess you could say I've always been an overachiever," Sabre muttered.

"Which is nothing to be ashamed of," she admonished. "You should be holding your head up with pride, not ducking it and trying to melt into the bolder."

He flushed with shame and met her eyes. "It's just that I've never had anyone talk to me about shape-shifting before."

"Did your folks not know about the traits you inherited?" she asked.

"I don't know. They passed away when I was three. I was raised in foster care."

Nodding, she seemed to be appraising him thoroughly while Sabre fought not to squirm. "If you wish to learn more, you're welcome to come back here. I'll answer any questions I can, and if I don't find the answer, we'll find you someone who does."

This time, it only took him a second to make up his mind about what he wanted. "Thank you. I'd like that."

"Wise choice."

He smiled at that, just about to ask another question when the crunch of leaves underfoot drew his attention. In the moonlight, he could just make out Professor Locklear approaching.

"So this is where you wandered off to?" his professor said.

"Yes, sir. Is it time to go?"

"Not yet, but soon. It's going to be a long drive back, so if you're hungry, you might want to grab something before we leave."

Sabre groaned and shook his head. "I'm still stuffed from dinner. The food was amazing, and I ate entirely too much of it."

"You're preaching to the choir there; my pants are starting to dig into me after everything I packed away."

"Which should teach you both moderation," Grace responded, her laugh ringing out over the dark meadow like the tinkle of a bell.

Even as Professor Locklear climbed up onto the rock beside him, Grace was sliding down hers, landing with a soft rustle of grass.

"Sabre, I will see you soon. But remember what I told you. Be proud of who you are, and know that this is a safe space where you don't have to hide, even with that one."

She'd inclined her head toward Professor Locklear and with another laugh, strode away.

"What was that all about?"

Sabre shrugged, suddenly feeling shy again with her gone. "We were just talking about her story."

"She has a way with words, doesn't she?"

"Yes, sir. Someday I hope to hold the attention of an audience that way."

"Well, you know, this is good practice if you ever have a story to share."

Shrugging again, he ducked his head, nibbling on his bottom lip as he eyed the ground, mumbling. "Ech, could be, I guess."

"Think about it. So, how'd you enjoy the story circle?"

Sabre jerked his head up, lips stretching into a smile. "It was amazing. I've never seen anything like it. There were so many amazing stories told and the conversations afterward were phenomenal. I expected it to be continuous reading, so I was pleasantly surprised when there was time to reflect between each storyteller and a chance for the audience to discuss their feelings about each story, the history some were steeped in, and the hilarity of others. The whole evening was...this huge hive of collective learning and discovery."

"Which is exactly the point," Professor Locklear remarked. "It isn't enough to listen. Real learning comes afterward. It's in the way each listener processes what they heard and how they share that knowledge with others. I was pleased you took part today. I hope you'll continue to do so back in my classroom."

Sabre nodded, actually looking forward to the opportunity. "I'm still not moving from my seat, though. I like it up there."

"Fair enough."

"I'd like to come to the discussion group, too, if the offer is still on the table. I really enjoyed talking to Ben, and if the others are anything like him, it will be an amazing learning experience."

"Of course it is, I wouldn't have invited you if I didn't think you could be a benefit to the group and it to you."

Turning, Sabre scooted to face his professor, fingers dancing through the air as he began to talk. "Thanks! I've been to all kinds of writing workshops and creative discussion groups, but even the open-mic nights aren't as inspiring as this was. I really had fun. Thank you for asking me to join you guys. I wouldn't have wanted to miss this for anything in the world. I can't believe how many ideas are spilling around in my head right now. I can't wait to get them all on paper. This was so...

Professor Locklear's lips meeting his own abruptly cut Sabre off, and he froze, shocked as his professor's fingers combed through his hair, his free arm sliding around his back, tugging him closer. Melting into the embrace, a surge of feelings and desire rushing through him, Sabre kissed back eagerly. Groaning, he deepened the kiss, a whirlwind of sensations flooding his body as Locklear's fingers stroked the back of his neck, making him shiver. He moaned, groping in the dark to feel Locklear's shirt beneath his fingertips and the silky softness of his hair. Time slipped away in a haze of feeling, tongues sliding against one another. He tasted the lingering sweetness of the strawberry ice cream the man had after dinner, the woodsy scent of his cologne filling his nose.

Panting, they finally drew back, a slow smile lifting Sabre's lips as he took in the rumpled, disheveled appearance of his professor.

Professor Locklear's eyes were wide, glancing around as if he wanted to assure himself no one had seen. "Shit! Fuck! I'm sorry. That shouldn't have happened. I don't know what came over me. Please, can you just forget I ever did that? I've never in my life crossed the line with a student like...

In an effort to get him to shut up, Sabre fisted both hands in his shirt and yanked him forward, kissing him thoroughly, half expecting to be shoved away. Instead, his professor growled, shuddered beneath his fingertips, and kissed him hard, nearly stealing the breath from his lungs. Every bit as intense as the first time, fingers scrabbled at the edges of clothes, tugging in a quest for skin. Sabre gasped at the first cold brush of the professor's hand along his ribs, a shiver running through him.

The teacher's back was warm beneath his hands, and the smoothness of Locklear's skin felt so good beneath his fingertips. Sabre moaned as his hair was gently tugged, forcing him to tip his head back, exposing his throat to teeth as the man nibbled down the side. Sabre grunted, desperate and needy as the older man pulled away, chest heaving.

Eye to eye, they stared at one another, Sabre too afraid to move and break the spell lest his professor go back to apologizing again. Sabre wasn't sorry in the slightest, and if anything, he wanted more of all those delicious feelings. Professor Locklear opened his mouth to say something, only to snap it shut when Ben's laughter reached their ears.

"Hey professor, Jonny fell asleep on a picnic table, and now Nazarene is trying to fall asleep on him," Ben declared.

All at once, the man was moving, and a cold wind whipped past Sabre, reminding him of how late it had gotten and how far the temperature had dropped.

"And that's the sign it's time to go," Professor Locklear remarked, striding away without a backward glance. Sabre remained where he was, blinking at Locklear's retreating back, wanting to call out but not wanting to make a scene. Hell, he wasn't even certain of what he would say if the man answered, so he left it alone, gathered his wits, and met Ben's curious gaze.

"Want to see something else before we go?" Ben asked. "It'll be quick, I promise. It's going to take Professor Locklear a few minutes to get Jonny moving, anyway. He's always a pain in the ass to wake up. I roomed with him last year, and man, his alarm would sound long enough to wake the dead before he rolled out of bed to shut it off. I made the mistake of turning it off once, and he was pissed because he ended up missing his first two classes."

"Damn."

"Pretty much. So you game?"

Sabre nodded and slid down, because it was easier to follow him and see whatever it was Ben wished to show him than try to figure out what those kisses meant. Walking past the fire, he could see a few people still lingered, the faint whispers of a story being told soared over the crackle of the fire. He paused, watching, listening a little.

"They'll be out here until dawn," Ben remarked, cutting through his thoughts. "We've stayed all night a few times, too, but only at the end of a semester. You should come."

"I will, I asked about the discussion group too."

"Good deal, I look forward to seeing you there."

At the edge of the field, Ben stopped at a grouping of totems Sabre hadn't noticed on the way in. Looking up, Sabre took note of the different animals there: bear, wolf, horse, bobcat, deer, moose, mountain lion, turtle, eagle, rabbit, and even a ferret.

"They're beautiful."

"They are, aren't they? But do you know what they stand for?" Ben asked.

Playing with the string on his hoodie, Sabre could only venture a guess. "Tribal spirit animals?"

"Not bad; you were paying attention. But they have a second significance too. They're..."

"The animal forms tribal members have been able to take over the course of the history of the tribe," Sabre remarked, reverence in his voice.

"Exactly."

"Grace said you're a brown bear."

Nodding, Ben threw an arm around Sabre's shoulders. "I am...and you are something I've never smelled before."

"Ferret," Sabre remarked.

"Nice. You know what this means, right?"

"I'm not entirely certain, no."

Ben chuckled and steered him toward the van. "It means you're one of us now, which means you'll be seeing a lot more of me."

Laughing, Sabre leaned into the warmth and strength of the embrace, grateful for the company on the long ride back to campus.

Chapter 8

HE WAS A FOOL, ONE hundred percent out of his goddamned mind to be doing this, but eyes trained on Sabre, Drax strode across the sprawling campus lawn toward the young man seated beneath a tree. Sabre's attention was entirely focused on the notebook in his hands, pen flying rapidly across the paper, tongue poking between his lips in what Drax was coming to realize was the picture of contemplation.

Kissing him had been a colossal mistake, but ignoring him afterward had been sheer torture. He'd stared at Sabre during classes, reminded of how his lips tasted of the tangerines passed around the circle. He woke hard and heavy the past few nights, the remnants of images in his head all of Sabre stretched out before a fire, the light playing off his skin the way it had danced across his face in the clearing.

It was wrong.

Damn him to hell, it was against his personal ethics, but he couldn't stop desiring the bright, inquisitive young man, who was starting to dominate his every thought.

College policy said that it was against the interests of the school for any teacher to date a student directly under their authority, defined as being in one of their courses, which Sabre would only be for a few more weeks. The policy also stated that faculty were strongly urged to be cautious about the perception other students might have, if the relationship became known, and faculty might be opening themselves up to accusations of favoritism. He hardly believed that would be an issue since Sabre wasn't even in his program. Hell, he was almost to graduation, and the rules for graduate students were different.

Dropping to the grass opposite him, Drax reached across the distance between them and placed his hand over the top of Sabre's notes when the younger man didn't so much as look at him. Wary black eyes met his, and Drax drank in their ebony depths.

"I've never done this before," Drax began.

"What, interrupted a student while they were working?"

Shaking his head, Drax tried for stern, even with the corners of his lips twitching. Smart, and a snarky personality. Oh, this was going to be fun.

"No, asked a student out."

The notebook fell from Sabre's grasp, and he didn't make a move to retrieve it.

"What?" Drax asked when no sound came from Sabre's slowly moving lips. "Did you think you could kiss me like that, and I wouldn't want to do it again?"

"If I remember correctly, you kissed me first."

"That I did, and I'd like to do it again."

"Are you sure you won't freak out afterward?" Sabre remarked, tearing his gaze away from Drax as he searched for his pen in the grass beside him.

Drax stilled his hand and scooted closer to slide the other beneath Sabre's chin, lifting so they were staring at one another again.

"I'm sorry for that; truly, I am. The whole moment was overwhelming, and I reacted badly. I shouldn't have walked away from you without a word, and I shouldn't have ignored you this week when you tried to speak to me."

"No, you shouldn't have, but you did. I've gotta tell you, that didn't feel so hot. I get it; I'm a student, and you're worried about appearances, but it's not like I go out of my way to seduce my teachers, so it's new to me too. I looked up school policy, just to see their stance on it."

Rubbing circles on the back of Sabre's hand with his thumb, Drax nodded. "So did I. It's only an issue for as long as you're in my class. After that, you get your degree and start graduate school, and no one can question a thing."

"Except maybe my grades."

"Heh, they'd be idiots. Besides, Grace has read your papers. If anyone could speak out to say your grades were warranted, it would be her. She practically raved over them and lamented the fact that you hadn't found us sooner. We might have had a shot at turning you into a Native Lit major."

"Who's to say I can't read and research the topics on my own? Just because I won't have the piece of paper doesn't mean I can't have the knowledge."

"True, and going that route won't put you in a position to have to take another of my classes, which would mean we'd be free to pursue a bit more of that kissing we were discussing earlier."

Sabre huffed and jerked his hand away before crossing his arms over his chest. "Only if we go out to dinner or something first."

"We can do that. In fact, I heard about this open mic on Friday night over at the Starlight Pub. Would you like to go?"

Grinning, Sabre nodded, and for the first time since he sat down, Drax felt as if he could truly relax. "Of course, we'll have to be discreet about any PDA until you graduate."

"I'm not really big on PDA, anyway. So, does this mean we're going out?"

"Well, first, how about you define going out. What do you see us doing? In case you didn't notice, I'm getting a bit too old for club nights and body shots."

When Sabre laughed, Drax likened it to music. He put his whole body into it, too, throwing his head back and exposing the elegant lines of his throat. His eyes closed, his shoulders shook, and the way he hugged himself made Drax wish he could feel it too.

"In case you haven't caught on yet, I have about as much interest in those things as you do, which is to say, none. I was thinking we could have coffee and dessert at the diner sometime and maybe go out for dinner, or order takeout, watch some movies or talk about the books we're reading. Perhaps we can put some music on one night, slow dance to a few songs. I like to go out on the trails when it's snowy and just walk. The forest in wintertime is the most beautiful thing in the world, everything sparkling and frozen. You could come, too, if you want. We can pack a couple thermoses of hot cocoa, throw a few shots of Baileys in, and pack a few sandwiches—make a day of it."

The idea floored him, unexpected, and yet, with a ton of potential. "A winter picnic? I like it. I couldn't think of a better way to spend a Saturday. I'm game. And yes, this means we're going out."

It took all of the restraint he possessed to keep from kissing Sabre breathless when he smiled, the intensity making his eyes sparkle

"Then I'll see you there," Sabre said as he checked his watch and began gathering up his things. "And on that note, I've got to get going."

"Art of the Motion Picture?"

"Yup, this class, we're discussing *The Wrestler*. That was one I'd never heard of before. It was positively superb, though I never imagined sports entertainers put their bodies through so much. I thought it was all fake, ya know?"

"I'm not exactly familiar with it, but perhaps we can discuss it more on Friday night. Did you want me to pick you up?"

"No, I'm going to walk; it's only four blocks from my dorm, and I love how the air smells this time of year."

"Thus, why you're sitting outside instead of in the library."

Shoving his things in his backpack, Sabre stood, stretching, rolling his neck until a loud crack was heard. "Who'd want to be inside on a day like today?"

"Sounds like you sat for too long."

"Yeah, and I've really neglected my workouts this week. I think I'll head down to the pool before bed, get a few hours of laps in. That way I can stretch my muscles and clear my head at the same time."

"Sounds like something else we can do together. I'm attempting to go more regularly, for much the same reasons. Sure is cheaper than constant visits to my chiropractor."

"I'm trying to avoid having to make an appointment," Sabre remarked as he rubbed the back of his neck. "Plus, it's the only thing that kept me from gaining the freshman fifteen my first year. I've kept up with it ever since. Could be I'll see you there. I'll warn you, though; I tend to go pretty late. Around eight or nine when there's no one else around."

Climbing to his feet, Drax brushed the dirt and grass cuttings from his pants, trying not to drool as he imagined Sabre in swim trunks.

"Sounds like the perfect time to avoid battling anyone else for a lane."

"Exactly."

Though he was fairly certain the real reason had more to do with Sabre's scar than wanting to avoid a crowd, he wasn't going to bring it up. Not when he'd just gotten lucky enough to get the man to agree to date him.

"Shit, I gotta run!" Whirling, Sabre tore off across the lawn, leaving Drax chuckling as he watched him go. Seemed like he was destined to make him late for motion picture class, something he'd have to be mindful of in the future. The last thing he wanted was to cause Sabre's grades to slip and jeopardize his ability to graduate and move on to the master's program. Not when he had some pretty clear-cut goals he was looking to accomplish.

Whistling, Drax headed for his office, thoughts of coffee and the stack of papers on his desk warring with the image of a soaked Sabre threatening to dominate his consciousness. Eight or nine o'clock swimming, huh? Perhaps it was a good thing he'd taken to keeping swim trunks in his office.

Chapter 9

FRIDAY, FINALLY! EAGERLY anticipating the open mic all week, Sabre was down to the last few hours of classes and an assignment that needed finishing, before he could grab a shower and get dressed. At the moment, however, he made his way along the wall toward the front of the room, intent on asking Professor Locklear a question that had been nagging him ever since he'd finished the book he'd sat up half the night reading.

Gripping, utterly fascinating, and tragic as all hell, he'd tossed and turned for almost an hour after he'd gone to bed, unable to get it out of his mind. As the last student filed out, Sabre approached the podium and brushed his hoodie back, having finally grown accustomed to not keeping his face shrouded when it was just him and Professor Locklear. Swimming beside the man for the past three nights had bolstered his confidence to be nearly naked around him.

"Hey," Professor Locklear remarked as soon as he saw him. "Are you looking forward to tonight? I sure am."

"Yes sir, unequivocally, but I do have a question for you."

"First, when we're alone, call me Drax. Professor is kind of weird, considering, and I'm not much into the whole sir thing; too many connotations, and to be honest, it sort of makes me feel old. I accept it as a term of respect in the classroom and during school functions, but when we're out together, we're contemporaries, understood?"

"Yes, s...err Drax."

"Much better. So, what was your question?"

"Well, I was wondering if you had time to explain something to me. It's really ambiguous in the books I've been reading and I thought you could put it in definitive terms."

"I can certainly try," Drax remarked as he closed the notebook on the lectern and stuffed it back in his briefcase. "So, what books are tripping you up?"

"Well, I just finished *They Call it Prairie Light, Essie's Story,* and *Where Courage is like a Wild Horse*, and the one thing I've struggled to get past was the way Native students were punished for using their own languages and for following the customs and traditions of their tribes. It felt like the people running the schools were trying to strip them of their identities, and in a documentary I watched online, many likened the government schools to sanctioned genocide."

It was impossible to miss the way Drax's jaw tightened and his fist clenched. "They were. It's a sore subject in my family, one of many reasons my great grandfather moved his family off the reservation, even if he worked himself into an early grave doing it."

"I'm sorry. I probably shouldn't have asked. I just, I don't understand why people would have continued to send their children there if they were going to be treated so horribly. I mean, the stories talked about beatings, humiliations, the cutting of their hair and the burning of their clothing to force them to adapt to white culture. Why not keep them home and build their own schools in their own communities?"

"They weren't given a choice. Either they willingly sent their children to the schools or their children were taken from them and sent to the schools anyway."

Drax began to pace, and Sabre watched his long strides carry him to the far side of the room and back again.

"Never apologize for asking questions," Drax remarked. "That's the only way to learn and to get past the culture of ignorance perpetrated more and more with every passing year. You know, when a person or a people protests something and tells you they don't like what's happening, what should happen is people listen and stop doing those things that are considered hurtful. Instead, what tends to happen in this country is people choose to ignore the actual problems in favor of complaining about how unlawful the protest is, even when it's peaceful. People today are still protesting the way hundreds of Native children are taken from their families each year and placed with non-Native foster families rather than certified Native ones. It's the government's way of continuing to erase the culture and history of our people, and every question that someone asks is an opportunity for knowledge and awareness to be spread."

"I...never would have considered it that way," Sabre remarked, after silently mulling over the professor's words. "I-I guess in a lot of ways, it's like the NFL protests, the kneeling during the anthem. People talk about how it's disrespectful to the flag and to the country's veterans while ignoring why it's happening in the first place. Most never consider the fact that the flag they hold so much reverence for, and pride in, might not have the same significance for those who haven't experienced the same freedoms and equality as they have."

"Precisely. And instead of addressing the concerns the protest was created to draw attention to, people keep the focus on the peaceful act of kneeling, instead of the violence in the streets. When you add in the fact that some of those kneeling in protest against racial injustice are doing so in jerseys bearing the racist logo of a team that has been asked to change their name time and time again and sometimes the hypocrisy is overwhelming."

"But how do we change that?"

"One person at a time," Drax said, the passion and conviction in his voice unmistakable. "We change it in classrooms, in discussion groups and forums, through interviews, stories, poetry, and song. We educate, we draw attention, we correct, and we don't stop until real change happens. Unfortunately, the wheels of change move even slower than the wheels of justice. And sometimes, there are far more steps backward than there are forward. That's why every student like you is a treasure. Someone who comes into my classroom with no real knowledge of the culture and the people, and instead of coasting through, chooses to seek the truth, educate themselves, and gain some enlightenment. ."

"Even if they're starting to call me your little pet," Sabre muttered.

Drax's eyebrows shot up. "When was this?"

"Just now, when I was passing the last few students, I heard one of them tell the other I was your little pet, always hanging around, sucking up after class. I thought about telling them it wasn't sucking up if you were asking questions you truly didn't know the answer to, but what would have been the point? They clearly don't have the concept of what school is all about and don't want to know, so why bother?"

"As unfortunate as it is, I agree."

Shuffling, Sabre shifted from one foot to the other, absently fiddling with the hoodie string. "I'd umm, better go. I've got a paper I wanted to finish before getting ready for tonight."

"We can always discuss it more this evening. In case I get there early, which would you prefer, a table or a booth?"

"I think a booth might offer more opportunities for conversation. All the tables seem to be adjacent to the stage. Speaking of which, I'm um, planning to read something tonight. I wrote a new poem, and I want to share it."

"Do I get a sneak preview?"

"Nope. You'll have to wait until tonight. Besides, I always end up tweaking things along the way. Sometimes just a line or two, but once, I actually arrived early and rewrote the whole thing."

Drax chuckled and shook his head. "Just remember, there is such a thing as over editing. You don't want to polish it so much that you wipe the shine off of it."

"I'll remember that," Sabre remarked, shouldering his pack and turning away.

"Hey, bring your appetite. I'm going to be starving by the time I get there, and I hate eating alone. Besides, I owe you supper for the way I acted after the story circle."

Half turning, Sabre glanced back over his shoulder and flashed Drax a grin. "Yeah, you do, and knowing how amazing their quesadillas are, I'm planning to have a few."

"You know what, that sounds good, I think I'll join you. Which do you prefer, the steak or the chicken?"

"Why don't we get a plate of each and share them? That way, neither of us has to choose."

"I like how you think. See you soon."

"You can count on it."

Chapter 10

DRAX STARED AT THE sway of Sabre's hips as he walked toward the stage. Briefly, he'd worried their conversations would be limited strictly to academia, and to his shame, he'd had a moment when he'd paused and considered if Sabre was using him to get ahead. Of course, that moment had quickly been followed by a reminder that one couldn't get much further ahead of the curve than Sabre already was. Fortunately, he'd been calm, cool, and collected by the time he arrived at the pub to find Sabre already seated in a booth, scribbling away in a notebook he'd stowed as soon as Drax sat. It was the same notebook he held in his hand as he climbed the three steps to the stage.

He kept his head down, Drax noted and studied the way Sabre angled his face away from the light, so his hair shadowed his scar. The more he worked to hide it, the more Drax wanted to know how he'd gotten it. What happened to make him isolate himself from everyone because of it? How much was fear of people's reactions, and how much was residual trauma? Maybe one day he'd get Sabre to tell him.

When Sabre began to speak, all other thoughts flew from Drax's mind.

"I'd, um, like to share a poem with you all tonight," Sabre said softly, only to receive a few whoops of encouragement from around the room.

It was mostly other college students, but Drax knew locals turned out, as well, sharing music and song and occasionally reading a story.

Even from his vantage point, Drax could see the papers fluttering slightly in Sabre's hand as he spoke into the mic again. "It's called 'Of Dreams and Ruined Fireflies.'

A hush fell over the room. Sabre licked his lips, lifted the notebook a little, throat working as he looked to swallow hard before launching into the poem.

Chain smoking dreams on the hood of my car,
We paint dragons in smoke against an azure sky
Waiting for the stars to chase the sun from too bright heavens.
Everything sparkles a little different after dark.
Tattered edges of glittery wings hide the fray in swirling neon.
We feign amusement in the face of scorn,
Crawl home and puke our sins in porcelain bowls,
The dregs of last night's misery oozing from our pores.
There's no escaping the long shadows that creep across our lives,
Shadowing the fall of all we once held dear.
Is there no end to the pantomime of life we endure?
This silent, black-and-white movie
Making us laugh at the broken clown.
Ashes fall like ruined fireflies,
A rain of white against tanned skin.
What careful disassembly of life the fire brings,
Reducing form to a barely recognizable mold, like our dreams.
The whispers of them still echo on nights like these,
When we lay beneath ancient moons,
Remembering all we'd hoped to be.

Lowering the notebook from his face, Sabre stepped back from the mic, but he never raised his eyes; instead, he sort of shuffled, one foot to the other, in the brief silence that followed his reading. Then the applause came, and a red bloom spread across his cheeks. Drax clapped enthusiastically and added his voice to the others whooping and cheering for the thoughtful words, but the one line that rolled over and over in Drax's mind was the final one.

Remembering all we'd hoped to be.

To him, it spoke of finality, the acceptance of lost dreams, and Drax wondered what Sabre was forced to let go of, and why. Did it have anything to do with his scar and how he'd gotten it: his parents' deaths, his upbringing in foster care, or a mix of all three? Had he wanted to be more than an author, some higher goal he felt was out of reach? If so, Drax wondered what that was and why, when he was still so young and able to do anything, was he relegating himself to something different. Or was Drax looking too deeply? Could the poem have not even been about Sabre but someone else, someone he'd known, someone he'd lost?

The applause followed Sabre back down the aisle as he returned to Drax, slipping onto the bench with his head down, that telltale blush still undeniably visible.

Drax reached across the table and ran his fingertips along Sabre's arm. "That was beautifully written."

"Thank you. I-I've been working on a short story, and this character has been in my head for a few weeks. The other night I could practically picture him sort of laid back, sprawled across the hood of his old muscle car, cigarette dangling from his lips as he stared at the stars and the city in the distance. It was so vivid, I had to write what he was thinking and feeling."

"Do you do that a lot—write from the perspective of the characters?"

He shrugged and laced their fingers together. "Sometimes; I mean, it's really up to them, when they speak to me, how they speak, and how clear it comes through."

"What do you mean, when they speak to you?"

"Just that the deeper I get into a piece of writing, the more acutely I can hear the conversations of the characters taking place inside my head. I can see them as vividly as if I were watching a movie. I don't have to think about it. The story flows as naturally as breathing and sometimes, the whole world melts away when I'm writing and I look up and realize the entire day has slipped away."

"When did you discover you loved to write?"

"Around the time I discovered books, like the two went hand in hand. I would read a story, and I wouldn't be able to get it out of my head. I would think about different things that might have happened to the characters, before, during, and after the parts I'd read and even how things could have gone differently. I'd write out my own twists and turns, different endings, different adventures. I didn't learn until later that it was an actual thing that people did and posted all over the Internet."

"Fanfiction."

"Exactly."

"I'd do it with movies too. It got to be part of the fun of watching them."

Drax chuckled, understanding completely. "We all need a guilty pleasure or two to get us through the monotony of a normal day."

"So what's yours?"

Sitting back a little, Drax stretched and felt a sense of contentment. How could he ever have expected this evening to be dull and filled with class material?

"Music. I've always loved jazz, the brassy sound of a trombone, the smooth silkiness of a saxophone. I took lessons for years, used to play in the high school marching band, college, too, but on the weekends me a few other members would get together and we'd play in a little lounge. I enjoyed it immensely."

"Do you still play?"

"From time to time. Not so much these past few years, between the course loads I've been teaching and everything that stems from it. I practice when I can, and sometimes I just break it out as a respite between papers. Play a few tunes and remember what it was like to be a kid with no responsibilities and a world of dreams. I thought briefly I might make a profession of it, and my folks would have supported that decision if that's where my heart had truly been, but the more I thought about it, the more I wanted to do something meaningful. Not to say that making people happy with music isn't a meaningful profession. It truly is, but I wanted to do something more one on one. I wanted to teach and influence people."

"I think that's really cool. Hopefully a time will come when I can sway people with my stories, engage their emotions and take them someplace they never imagined existed."

"I have no doubt you can do anything you set your mind to, especially if you put into them the same hard work and dedication I've seen you pour into your classwork."

Drax was treated to a smile as Sabre gently squeezed his fingers.

"Thanks."

"Would you care to get out of here? Go someplace more private where we can talk some more, perhaps over a mug of tea and some pie?"

"Pie, huh? What kind?"

"Caramel Apple," Drax replied. "I've got whipped cream in a can and some apple cinnamon tea to sweeten the deal."

"Hell, you had me at caramel apple," Sabre remarked as he stood, all but tugging Drax out of the booth with him.

"Eager much?"

Sabre just licked his lips and gave him such a wickedly sinful grin that Drax's cock gave a twitch at the thought of where he'd like Sabre to stick that tongue. Hand in hand they headed for the door, unmindful of the few curious stares around them.

Chapter 11

SABRE ALLOWED DRAX to lead him through the darkness of the living room toward the light left burning in the kitchen. Small and cozy, with a round table sitting in a corner alcove and set with two chairs, the room boasted a long line of gleaming wooden cabinets and a brown granite countertop. Both the refrigerator and the range were made of shiny black metal, with containers made of similar material lining the walls along the counter. Looking closely, Sabre made note of the fact they were all labeled.

The whole space was tidy, and Sabre took it all in as Drax filled a kettle with water and set it on the stove, a soft click preceding the lighting of the burner. Not for the first time did Sabre lament the fact that the ranges in student housing were all electric, at least, for those who were lucky enough to have one of the rare studio apartments that had them. Most relied on microwaves and coffee pots in dorm rooms where hotplates and toaster ovens were banned.

"Have a seat. I'll have everything ready in a moment. I'm going to heat the pie a little and get the caramel melting a bit."

Sabre's moan slipped from his lips. Watching Drax place a couple tea bags in mugs and pull the pie pan from the fridge gave him a wonderful opportunity to study how at ease he looked here. He was confident in the classroom, too, pacing and talking with grand, animated gestures when he spoke, but here, there was a relaxed and casual air about him. It wasn't long before Drax was sliding a slice of pie beneath his nose, alongside a steaming mug of tea.

"Wow! That smells delicious."

"Thanks. I wish I could take credit for the pie, but my culinary skills are pretty basic. I got this from the bakery in town."

"Oh man, I love that place."

The first bite gave an amazing burst of flavors; the apple and the buttery caramel was damn near decadent. Sabre let his eyes drift shut as he took a sip of tea to wash it down. Slowly, piece by piece, he took his time enjoying the flakiness of the sugar-dusted crust and the tenderness of the apples until his plate was empty, and he'd finished the final swallow. Only then did he realize Drax's plate sat unfinished across from him while the man just stared, mouth half open.

"What?" Sabre asked, reaching for a napkin and dabbing his lips, hoping he hadn't made a mess with the whipped cream.

"I have never seen someone make eating pie look so goddamned sensual," Drax remarked as he leaned closer, reached out, and brushed at the corner of Sabre's mouth. "You missed a spot."

Now it was Sabre's turn to stare as Drax stuck his finger in his mouth, sucking off the dab of cream.

A low chuckle came from Drax, who quickly cleaned his plate and collected the dishes, carrying them to the sink. Sabre followed, pressing himself against Drax's side and kissing his neck, drawing a low moan from him.

"I've wanted to do that all night," Sabre murmured, feeling Drax shiver beneath his lips.

"Oh, really? I'm not sure I'm convinced."

Licking a stripe of skin, Sabre ran his tongue along the side of Drax's throat, down to his shoulder, nipping lightly at the place where they met, grinning when Drax exhaled raggedly.

"Convinced yet?" Sabre muttered.

"Not...quite."

"Mmm, really?"

He slid a hand into Drax's hair, fingers tangling in the strands as he angled his head away, giving him better access to kiss his neck and throat, nuzzling and pressing tightly to him.

"Fuck!"

The strangled sound seemed torn from Drax as he spun, crushing his lips against Sabre's. Just like back on the rock, it was electric. His skin ached for every touch as Drax's fingers wormed their way beneath his shirt. Chest to chest against the counters, they kissed like they needed the taste of one another to breathe. Shirts were tugged from jeans, hair was groped and even pulled a little. Hips rolled, pressing straining, jean-clad erections together, sending jolts of pleasure rocketing through them.

They tore apart with gasps and groans, panting, fingers still stroking one another's face, arms, and back, needing that connection as they tried to reign themselves in.

"We should continue this somewhere more comfortable, preferably with a lot less clothing," Drax urged.

"I like that idea."

"Good, because I want to touch you without getting all tangled up in cloth to do it."

Grinning, Sabre nodded, then leaned in to kiss him again, gently, slowly, and a lot less desperately. "I-I don't mind getting naked, but..."

Drax tenderly brushed a strand of hair back from Sabre's face. "Just touching tonight, nothing more; we'll just make one another feel good."

Sabre shivered at the feeling and pressed into the soft touch, enjoying the way Drax caressed him. "That sounds really, really good."

Cupping the back of his neck, Drax held him in place while kissing him deeply. Groaning, Sabre slid both hands beneath his shirt, running them upward until he felt the pebbled firmness of Drax's nipples hardening more beneath his fingertips. He felt Drax's sharp intake of breath, so sudden it nearly left him breathless too. Then Drax's hand was cupping his ass, rocking his hips so their lower bodies were pressed together again, and Sabre needed friction like never before.

Panting, he broke the kiss, vision fuzzy, head spinning. "Please."

"God, yes, come on."

Drax's hand closed around his, pulling, propelling him toward the door. Fumbling, they hurried down a short hall, spilling into Drax's room with a burst of laughter. Sabre felt giddy with anticipation as he tugged at Drax's sweater, yanking it up and over the man's head, tangling it around Drax's arm a bit before depositing it on the floor. Not like Drax was doing much better—he'd managed to undo the button on Sabre's jeans as Sabre undid the top two buttons of his flannel shirt and yanked it off, quickly followed by his T-shirt and Drax's turtleneck.

Shoving Drax's hands away, Sabre removed his own jeans and boxers, nearly tripping over the ends as he stepped out. His eyes were on Drax's cock—the first good look he got at it. Seeing him in swim trunks hadn't done him justice. Thick and uncut was the first thing Sabre noticed; the second was that Drax's average size curved to the left, with a mushroom-shaped head that looked delicious.

Drax's firm grip steadied him, pushing to get Sabre to move until the backs of his knees hit the edge of the bed, and he sank onto the plush surface. Drax urged him to lie back, and Sabre complied as Drax slid up beside him and touched the table lamp, plunging them into darkness.

In all his life, this was the most intimacy he'd had, lying molded against another man in the darkness of a bedroom, gently running his fingers down his side and arm.

Tugging him closer, Drax kissed him, hand stroking down his hair, over his shoulders, and Sabre was more than happy to explore him in return. Skimming his fingers along Drax's side, he soon discovered a ticklish place near his hip and a second one halfway up his ribs.

"Really," Drax growled, but Sabre could hear the laughter and playfulness in his voice.

"Oh yeah," Sabre remarked, tickling deliberately now, making Drax wiggle and squirm. Straddling him, Sabre groaned as their cocks touched, sliding against one another as Sabre tangled his fingers in Drax's hair and kissed him thoroughly. Drax's hands slid down his back, stroking, caressing, holding him tight in a firm grip, the only warning Sabre got before Drax bucked his hips and rolled them.

"Guess you wanted to be on top," Sabre muttered.

"Tired of you having all the fun, you mean," Drax remarked, before kissing him thoroughly. While Sabre's head was still reeling, Drax moved lower, doing wicked things with his tongue when he got to Sabre's pecks.

Gasping, Sabre pressed against Drax's head, alternately trying to hold his face there and shove it away.

"Like that?"

"I-its...mmm...too much, not enough, fuck..." Drax chuckled, his breath hot against Sabre's skin. He swirled his tongue around the puckered flesh and Sabre's eyes rolled back as he quivered. When Drax blew across the wet skin,

Sabre groaned, and when he scraped his teeth against Sabre's nipple, he arched off the bed, crying out for more, grateful when Drax seemed happy to oblige.

Running his palms over Drax's shoulders, he felt the strength there and in Drax's hands as he held him down, making everything heady with pleasure. Shoving, he got Drax to roll on his side and tugged him upward so they could kiss again. His balls ached and his cock was weeping, and as he gently closed his fingers around Drax's, he could tell he was leaking too. Spreading the slick precum over the head with his thumb, he worked it up and down the shaft, twisting his wrist just a little at the end, drawing a groan from Drax.

"Lube..." Drax groaned, and Sabre let go so Drax could roll away to get it. He was back moments later; the click of the top flicking open was soon followed by Drax coating both of them in the cool slick. Wrapping his hand around both their lengths, he pressed them together, stroking slowly. Reaching down, Sabre joined him, nipping and sucking at Drax's shoulder as the delicious friction drew moans and sighs from both of their throats.

The pace was perfect, almost agonizingly slow at first, before Drax upped the tempo. They kissed, messy and rough, gasping into each other's mouths when the bed began to rock with their frantic movements as Drax took things a bit faster.

"Good, so, so good," Sabre cried out, keening at the glide of Drax's fist and cock. Shaking, he clung, matching him stroke for stroke, pressing tighter, long, drawn-out groans pouring from him.

"God, I can't. Not gonna last. Oh, oh fuck," Drax cried, and Sabre felt the man tense, pulses of cum erupting from his cock as he clung to him. Cum splattered Sabre's chest—hot, dirty—and with a cry, Sabre added to the mess.

He lost track of how long they lay there, clinging to one another, panting, hands lazily stroking until sensitivity and discomfort finally brought things to a halt. Drax pressed a tender kiss to his temple and another to the corner of his mouth before Sabre kissed him full-on and stroked his hair.

"Will you sleep here tonight?" Drax murmured against his lips.

"Oh yeah, don't wanna move."

"Good. I have to, though. I'll be right back with something to clean us up."

"Mmm-kay," Sabre muttered, flopping over on his back. Content and relaxed, he must have started dozing off, because the feel of a warm, wet cloth against his chest startled him.

"Shhhh, relax," Drax whispered, cleaning the mess from his skin. Sighing, Sabre held still until he was done, cuddling to Drax as soon as he rejoined him in the bed. Wrapped in the warmth of Drax's arms with his back pressed to Drax's chest, he closed his eyes and drifted off to sleep.

Chapter 12

YAWNING, DRAX STRETCHED and rolled over, intent on kissing a path down Sabre's spine. Instead, he felt only vast emptiness. Lifting his head, he eyed the spot where Sabre had been the night before and was dismayed he'd left without a word. What was even more astonishing was he hadn't felt it happening. It had been a long time since he'd slept so deeply. Fuck. He felt the space, cold beneath his hand, a telltale sign that it was a while since Sabre left. Lying there, he reflected back on the evening, trying to figure out what he could have said and done to cause Sabre to do the walk of shame. Surely, if he'd had someplace to be, he would have said something, wouldn't he? Which just further confirmed for Drax that he'd somehow fucked up.

Shit.

Babbberbabberbabberbabberbabber

Huh?

Lifting his head, Drax turned it toward the sound, jaw dropping open at the sight of a gold and black ferret on the pillow. Their eyes met and the animal's ears twitched. Head bobbing, the ferret's nose wiggled before he whirled around and scurried off the side of the bed. It only took Drax a split second to connect the gold and black hues with the tones of Sabre's hair.

"No, wait!" Drax cried out, scrambling from the bed to close the door before the ferret could escape the room. It helped that he'd gone to bed on the side closest to it. Otherwise, he doubted he'd have been able to beat the ferret in his haste to escape. In a flash, the little critter darted beneath the bed. Drax took a deep breath and rubbed the back of his neck, cautioning himself to slow down and approach him calmly. Flipping up the edge of the comforter, he laid beside the bed. In the weak light of early morning, it was difficult to see much more than a shadow hunched against the wall.

"Hey, Sabre, listen, please. There's really no reason to hide. It's fine, I promise. I know about shapeshifters. To be honest, I'm kind of jealous. I've always wondered what it would be like to be able to change forms and look at you. That's a pretty cool one, reminds me of the two little thieves on the old *Beastmaster* movies."

Babbberbabberbabberbabberbabberbabber

"I'm sorry, I wish I could understand what you just said to me. Hope you're not cussing me out," Drax remarked as he reached a hand out to try to touch him. Unfortunately, he was too far away. "Come out, please? I'd really like to talk."

Babber babber

"Preferably in English, if that would be all right with you. I'm hoping for a two-way conversation, and right now, I'm feeling like I'm at a bit of a disadvantage."

Babber

Drax watched him uncoil, bobbing his way forward until warm, soft fur brushed against his fingers.

Babberbabberbabberbabberbabber

Holding perfectly still, Drax didn't want to do anything that might spook him or send him fleeing back beneath the bed again. Sabre brushed against his arm, rubbing his furred side along the length of it before cuddling beside Drax's shoulder.

Babber

"Thank you."

Babber

Slowly, Drax reached up and stroked his fur, rewarded with several more babbers and some nuzzling. He rolled carefully, holding his hands open for Sabre, pleased when he climbed in. Placing him on the bed, Drax sat back on his heels, eyeing him expectantly, until the ferret stretched, joints popping as its body contorted, lengthened and changed, the fur slowly giving way to flesh.

"Hey there. You okay?"

Sabre nodded, a red flush covering his cheeks as he rolled off the other side and began searching for his clothes. "I am so, so sorry. That's never happened before. I must have dreamed about shifting or something. I don't know. I didn't think that could happen. You won't tell anyone will you?"

Shoving himself to his feet, Drax stalked around the bed to catch Sabre's wrist, stopping him from pulling on his jeans.

"Of course not. But I don't want you to go either. There's no reason for it and nothing to be sorry for. Didn't you hear what I said? I think it's pretty goddamned amazing. I think you're pretty goddamned amazing, and this thing between us is something I'm looking forward to exploring. So please, come sit down on the bed with me and let's talk, okay?"

Sabre bit his lip, the sight prompting Drax to run his finger across it, urging him to let it go before he actually did damage.

"Please," Drax urged, cupping his chin, refusing to let him look away.

"Okay."

Drax breathed out a heavy sigh and drew Sabre into a hug, pressing a kiss to the top of his head. "Thank you."

Leading Sabre back to the bed, Drax urged him to lie back, spooning against him much as he had the night before and holding him there.

"Professor Windtalker said you knew about shifters and were okay with it. I should have listened."

Drax rubbed lazy circles on Sabre's arm and back, hoping that would help him settle. "Yes, you should have. What happened this morning was nothing to get upset about. In fact, it was far better than what I thought happened when I first woke up. "

"What do you mean?"

"Just that I thought you'd left, and I was lying there wondering what I'd done wrong to make you go."

"I really enjoyed the evening, all of it, though falling asleep in your arms was one of the really, really good parts."

"Yeah, what were some of the others?"

"The conversations. I love that I can talk movies with you and not just the classic ones but the old and obscure, too, and I'd love to hear you play the sax one day, especially if it's a Christmas song. I loved Kenny G's Christmas album."

"I'm pretty partial to that one myself. Which song is your favorite?"

"'Have Yourself a Merry Little Christmas.'"

"Oh yeah, there's a tone and mood to that one that as soon as I hear it, I start thinking about hot cocoa and watching the snow falling past the window."

Sabre chuckled. "I'd much rather listen to it out on a trail, the snow falling around me, clinging to branches. There's a sort of hush to the forest in winter, a stillness that's almost surreal. I feel like I can walk, wander, and clear my head of everything."

"I wouldn't mind joining you, as long as I was appropriately garbed in about three layers."

Sighing, Sabre cuddled closer. "I love the snow, and I love being able to shift out there and play in it."

Laughing, Drax could just picture it, the little ferret tunneling through a dune before popping up to scamper across the pristine snow. Sabre laughed, too, and Drax was pleased to feel his muscles weren't as tense as they'd been when he first lay down.

"I'd love to see that. I bet you'd be absolutely adorable frolicking around, chattering to the squirrels and chipmunks."

"Not sure they'd agree; usually they're cussing me out. I'm pretty sure they think I'm out to steal their food or something."

"Ahh."

"Yeah, you should see them, indignant as all hell, chattering at me from a log like they want to kick my ass. If I ever decide to write a children's book, I swear some of them are going to end up as characters."

"Guess you have to take the inspiration where you can find it."

"Exactly, and out in the woods, I can just be me."

"In here you can do that too," Drax sought to assure him. "I want you to think of this as a safe space. If you want to shift, then shift. If you want to lie on me, then I'll be happy for the cuddles. Just, don't hide, okay? Shifting is nothing to be ashamed of."

"Professor Windtalker said that too."

Laughing, Drax dragged his hand up Sabre's back, eliciting a pleased little moan. "I'd learn to listen to her if I were you. Trust me on that. It's never good to ignore her. I found that out the hard way."

"I never would have taken you for being stubborn."

"Wait long enough, you will."

Sabre chuckled, resting his cheek against Drax's chest.

"How did you find out you could shape-shift?" Drax asked as he lazily carded his fingers through Sabre's hair.

Sabre moaned, turning his head just a little and sighing when Drax's fingers brushed a sensitive spot. "Mmmm, it was completely by accident. I was starting at a new school. I was really anxious, all day, I couldn't concentrate. My skin itched, and I couldn't sit still. Everything felt too tight, constricting, and I ..."

Sabre sighed and let out another soft little hmm preening a bit as Drax continued to stroke. "God that's nice."

Drax grinned. It was good to see Sabre so relaxed. "So what happened then? What did you do?"

"I bolted out of class and ran from the building down to this little creek in the woods that bordered the property. I remember crying my eyes out over everything, really. So many things in my life were so overwhelming, and I didn't have anyone to talk to. My new foster family seemed nice, but I'd only been there a few days, so the jury was still out on them."

"That had to have been hard, to change families that way and never quite be able to know where you belonged," Drax murmured.

"It sucked, but it had become my normal."

"I'm sorry."

"So am I."

He quieted then, stilling under Drax's fingers and seeming to draw in on himself, as if he were trying to make himself smaller.

"Hey. Please don't shut down on me. I'd like to hear the rest of it," Drax urged, keeping his voice soft and slow like he was speaking to a spooked animal, which, in a way, he realized, he really was.

Sabre sighed, and for a moment, Drax wasn't sure he'd comply, but then Sabre spoke again. "I started flinging stones in the water, and after that, everything gets hazy. I remember shaking so hard I could hardly pick up the stones, let alone close my hand tight enough around them to get a good grip for throwing. Then everything sort of tilted sideways, and the next thing I knew, I was on the ground, and the scent of dirt was sharp and rich in my nose, more pungent than it had ever smelled to me."

"Your senses had dialed up, hadn't they?"

"Yeah, like ratcheted way the hell up, but before I could give much thought to it, I couldn't see. My clothes were pooled around me, and it took several seconds to scramble and squirm my way out. Of course, I promptly tripped over my feet and fell snout first into the creek. Coughing, sputtering, I floundered around, dripping water everywhere, but when the surface finally cleared, I saw what I'd become. At that point, I panicked, tried to whirl around, tripped on my tail, and fell backward into the creek. Scrambling out, I cut a paw on a piece of glass and had a bit of a meltdown. "

"I'm not sure I'd have handled it any differently," Drax remarked, fighting the urge to chuckle. "So how did you return to your human form?"

"Well, after I freaked out, I was so exhausted from the shifting and from falling all over the place, I just lay there half in and half out of the creek, feeling pretty muddy and disgusting. The only thing I wanted was to be human again and go back to class; that's all I kept thinking, over and over, and suddenly, I was, but I was a mess—my clothes were kind of muddy from where they'd fallen off me, and there was muck smeared on my skin."

"Not a good way to return to the classroom."

"No, it wasn't, but I had an incredible teacher, who was more concerned about why I'd run off in the first place. I couldn't tell her I'd turned into a ferret, but I could tell her I'd been extremely overwhelmed. She left her para-educator with the class and walked me to the nurse, helped clean the mud off me, and talked to me about what I felt."

"Sounds like someone who really cared about her students."

"Oh yeah, she became one of my favorite teachers, once I had time to adjust. She called my foster mom and told her what happened, and she came to get me, worked it out with the school so I didn't have to go for the rest of the week. Instead, she stayed home with me, helped me get used to their house, their routine, let me get to know her, and her husband was awesome about it too. When he came home from work each day, he'd spend one-on-one time with me, making sure I got to know him and learn what I could expect from them. It turned out to be a wonderful place to live; it totally sucked when I got moved six months later. They'd called it a transitional home. I never understood why they couldn't find a long-term placement for me. It wasn't like I was a troublemaker. It was brutal getting bounced around. I never settled into a place easily, so every move was stressful, and I was always on edge. As I'd settle in, they'd move me and the cycle of readjustment would start all over again."

While he talked, Drax never stopped caressing him, pleased that Sabre was feeling comfortable enough to tell his story. On one hand, he didn't want to push for something that wasn't being offered, but on the other, he wanted to know, felt like he needed to know, so he didn't accidentally trigger something. Tread carefully, his inner voice whispered, so Drax pulled Sabre into a hug and kissed his forehead.

"What was your longest placement?" Drax finally asked.

"The last one. I got to spend my junior and senior years of high school with Mr. and Mrs. Bouchard. There was another foster child in their home as well, Tanya. She was a year younger than me, and then there was Grandmeme Bouchard who lived there too. She's the one who'd sit us down with snacks and tea after school and talk to us about our day before we started our homework, right there at the table. She said it was so we couldn't get distracted, but I think it was because she enjoyed the company while she cooked. She even taught us how to make a few meals so we could feed ourselves right when we were out on our own. That was really important to her—that we knew how to make a balanced meal, not crap from a box."

Chuckling, Drax gave him a squeeze. "Sounds like my grandmother. That's pretty much how she puts it too. The last time she visited me, she lamented about the contents of my kitchen and made me drive her to the grocery store to do some proper shopping."

They laughed together, and Drax shivered as Sabre pressed a kiss to his chest.

"I love them," Sabre remarked. "I go home every chance I get. Holidays are amazing because other foster kids they've had over the years come back too. It's the one place we found that we all belong. And after what happened to my face... I don't think I could have handled another move."

His voice trailed off, plunging them both into silence. This was the moment Drax had been waiting for, and yet, feeling Sabre tremble, he didn't want to press. Instead, he waited, hoping Sabre would continue.

"My scar. It...it wasn't an accident," Sabre muttered.

"I didn't think it was with the way you kept it hidden and reacted when I commented on it. Who hurt you?"

"I don't know his name; he ran off when Tanya maced him. We were walking home from her play rehearsal since our folks had to go to a dinner that night, a work thing. This guy grabbed her purse as we were walking past him, but she had it slung across her chest, so it didn't come off when he yanked. He started pulling at her, and I shoved him and tried to get him to stop. The second time I shoved him, he hit the wall and let go. I grabbed her hand, and we started to run, but he caught up, spun me around, slashed at me with the glass. Tanya was able to pull out the mace our father had given her and sprayed him. Then she took my hand and ran, pulling me along. She got me to the corner grocery store down the block from our house, and Mr. Renaldo called for an ambulance. Then he called our folks, locked the door in case we were followed, got out his gun, and protected us until the police and EMTs came."

"You guys were lucky to have each other that night."

"I know. The one thing I have always been thankful for is that I was the one who got hurt, not her."

"Spoken like a true big brother."

Sabre raised his head, seeing his gaze. "Blood doesn't make families; love and trust do."

"Ain't that the truth."

"Can I ask you a question?"

"Of course, especially after everything you've told me. And for the record, you don't have to ask permission to ask a question. If you want to know something, just say so."

A slow smile spread across Sabre's lips, brightening his eyes and chasing away some of the sadness Drax saw there.

"How long you've known about shapeshifters?"

"Most of my life. I was four or five the first time I saw someone shift. Her form was that of a red-tailed hawk. I remember asking her if it hurt and what it was like to take another form, and she described this view of the mountains where the clouds were so low that the peaks and the tops of the pines stood up through them. She said the first brush of the sun turned them purple, and that it was sad that down here all we could see was the pink and gold. After that, I started drawing pictures that way in my art classes."

"That does sound beautiful."

Drax's stomach growled, loud enough that Sabre raised an eyebrow at him.

"Maybe we should continue this conversation over breakfast," Sabre suggested.

Drax chuckled. "Good idea. I make a kick-ass omelet, and I'm relatively certain there's some bacon in there too. I've got blackberries and bread for toast if you want some."

As if in answer, Sabre's stomach let out a growl of its own.

"I'll take that as a yes."

Chapter 13

THE TINY FIREPLACE in Drax's living room was more than enough to keep the space cozy and warm. Dangling from Drax's shoulder in his ferret form, Sabre babbered contently as he read from the book on Drax's knee, while Drax graded the papers on his lap. Two glasses of wine sat mostly empty on the coffee table in front of him, their empty plates a reminder of the cheese-stuffed Salisbury steaks and mashed potatoes Sabre had made them for dinner.

Though odd and a little bit awkward at first, rummaging around in Drax's kitchen for ingredients while the other man sat at the table, drowning under midterm papers; Sabre had found everything with little issue, despite Drax's insistence they just get takeout.

"I'm sorry we can't just kick back and relax tonight," Drax remarked before Sabre reminded him that he needed to study for finals himself. The fact that they could enjoy being together without needing to talk was just another plus to their relationship.

In the three weeks since Drax had woken to find him shifted on the pillow, Sabre spent almost as many nights in this room as he did in the library. Some nights, they cooked together before they settled down to work; other nights Drax cooked for them, something Sabre reminded him of when Drax tried to protest Sabre doing the same. Sharing something so simple with someone else was nice. The ease with which they moved around one another in the kitchen had surprised him too, but Sabre loved the nights best. Lying in the dark, curled to Drax's side, talking over a wide variety of topics, Sabre felt a connection unlike any he'd ever known in his life. Not that it was all easy or perfect.

Three days after the open mic he'd had a panic attack in Drax's classroom, the violence depicted in images Drax showed to accompany one of the stories reminded him too much of his own injury. Fortunately, it happened toward the end, and he'd managed not to freak out completely. Teeth dug into the cloth of his sleeve, he'd huddled, face pressed to the desk, trying not to make a sound. At some point, after everyone left, Drax realized that Sabre hadn't moved from his seat and he came to check on him. Unfortunately, Grace walked into the room as Drax was kissing his forehead and talking soothingly in an attempt to settle him down.

Once he was okay, they both received a lecture from her about the importance of keeping their relationship on campus completely aboveboard until Sabre finished with Drax's class. They'd both assured her they would. Here, in the privacy of Drax's home, however, they were free to be themselves and enjoy one another in whatever manner they saw fit.

Stretching, Sabre babbered and slunk down Drax's arm, flopping onto the couch cushions and shifting. The casual nudity that came from flipping back and forth between forms was becoming easier for Sabre. He'd discovered right after that first breakfast together that Drax enjoyed cuddling and petting him in his ferret form.

"It's calming—the feel of your fur beneath my fingers is like a touchstone. I don't mind at all if you want to stay that way. I can always prop your book up for you while you read."

Still, it was weird, at first, and Sabre wasn't really sure how he felt about it. Each day left him more and more at ease, though, and tonight, the only thing on his mind was a hot cup of coffee as he walked naked past Drax.

A hand on his hip stilled him, and he looked down to see hunger and need in Drax's eyes.

"Come 'ere," Drax growled, tugging him around until Sabre's cock was bobbing right in front of his face. Grinning, he flicked out his tongue, running it along Sabre's length.

"Gaaa!"

"I love when I can render you speechless," Drax murmured, his breath warm against his dick. Before Sabre could fire off a smart-assed remark, Drax sucked on the head, drawing a long moan from him as he closed his eyes. Grasping, one hand found Drax's shoulder, the other his hair.

Drax hummed, and Sabre felt the vibration rocket through him as his knees threatened to buckle. Gripping Drax's shoulder, he held on as Drax swirled his tongue around him.

Babberbabberbabbber

Drax froze and Sabre groaned, forced his eyes open to look down at the shit-eating grin Drax was giving him.

"Did I just make you babber?"

Sabre could feel his face heating up and licked his lips, smirking down at him. "I think you know the answer to that. Now how about you make me come?"

The growl his words tore from Drax was almost as sexy as the way he sucked him back into his mouth and hummed loudly as his head began to bob. On every downward motion, he'd hum, drawing out the sound as he slid his mouth up his length, changing the tone and frequency. All Sabre could do was cling, gasping, shuddering, the occasional babber mingling in as Drax continued ratcheting up the levels of pleasure, until, with a shuddering groan, Sabre came hard.

Drax sucked him through it, drawing mews and half-choked sobs.

"Mmm, too much. Oh, my god. I can't. No more," Sabre chocked out, sagging with relief when Drax stopped and tugged him into his lap, engulfing him in a hug.

"Feel better?"

Words were too hard, his heart was pounding and tiny tremors were still shooting through his body. "Mmm hmm."

He could have melted on the spot when Drax started stroking his hair and pressing featherlight kisses against his temple.

"You're so goddamned hot when you're flying apart for me," Drax whispered, drawing another shiver from Sabre, who clung, waiting for his heartbeat to slow again.

Everything felt better. The headache that had been threatening to start was just about gone now. That's what had gotten him moving toward the kitchen for coffee in the first place. Cuddling closer, he let out a contented little sigh.

Drax kissed the top of his head. "We should call it a night; it's already after one."

"No wonder I was starting to get a headache. Was gonna get a coffee, but you pretty much took care of that for me."

"All the more reason we should go lie down. It won't do you any good to be in pain in the morning when you have to take your midterms. Besides, you know the material forward and backward, so you'll do just fine. As soon as we both get through this, I'm treating you to a weekend away. We can take a drive through the mountains, take in the sights, stay at a bed and breakfast and investigate the museums and artisan shops. There are a few fantastic bookstores up that way too. It's been several years since I've taken off and driven that stretch. It would be a great way to de-stress and allow you numerous new experiences."

"God, that sounds good. I can't remember the last time I was so stressed about exams."

"Probably because these are the final ones, at least for this degree program. It's always harder when you're closer to a goal. You start to worry it will all be snatched away. I got so worked up about the final exam of my undergraduate years that I stayed up until about four in the morning the night before, guzzling coffee and popping NoDoz. I ended up puking my guts out and passing out on the bathroom floor. It was a good thing I had an understanding professor. She let me take the exam after I got out of the infirmary. I still didn't do as well as I could have, though. I don't want to see that happen to you."

"Then I guess I'd better listen when you tell me it's time to call it a night."

"Yup, so why aren't you moving?"

"You're warm, and this feels good."

"You feel good. Come on, let's pack up and go to bed, and maybe make out a little," Drax urged, though he didn't make any effort to move him.

"Hmm, don't wanna move."

"Neither do I, but if we sleep out here, neither of us will be able to move in the morning."

Wrinkling his nose at the memory of the one and only night they'd fallen asleep out there, Sabre had to agree. Slowly, he reluctantly climbed to his feet and stretched until his back popped. After gathering up his books and note cards, notebooks, and highlighters, he tucked them neatly back in his battered old backpack. It was patched in places with pieces of denim and decals, the original material almost completely covered with cartoon characters, slogans, symbols, and emoji signs. It didn't even have a shape anymore. It was past time to retire it, and he would, just as soon as the semester was over. Kick things off after the holiday break with a new bag, new course load, new degree program, and of course, his new and growing relationship. Placing the bag by the door, he eyed Drax through sleepy eyes, watching him place everything back on his desk in neat piles. Stepping up beside him, he slid an arm around Drax and kissed his cheek.

"Can we pass on the making out tonight?" he asked. "I think I'd rather shift and curl up in your arms."

Drax chuckled and stroked the back of his head. "Yeah, we can make that work, my little Ta Weezo."

"Mmm, thank you. God that feels good. "Ta Weezo, huh? I like that, a lot—far, far better than teacher's pet." Grinning, Sabre brushed a kiss across Drax's lips. "Not a teacher's pet, but you can pet me all you want."

And with that, he shifted, curling into Drax's arms and snuggling close.

"Then pet you I will," Drax remarked, running fingertips through his fur in a gentle massage as Sabre's eyelids grew heavy. One soft, babber of appreciation later, the arms of sleep claimed him.

Also by Layla Dorine

Guitars and Family
Guitars and Cages
Guitars and Choices

Standalone
Ta Weezo's Blues

Watch for more at https://layladorine13.wixsite.com/layladorineauthor.

About the Author

LAYLA DORINE lives among the sprawling prairies of Midwestern America, in a house with more cats than people. She loves hiking, fishing, swimming, martial arts, camping out, photography, traveling, and visiting museums and haunted places.

Layla got hooked on writing as a child and she hasn't stopped writing since. Hard times, troubled times, the lives of her characters are never easy, but then what life is? The story is in the struggle, the journey, the triumphs and the falls. She writes about artists, musicians, loners, drifters, dreamers, hippies, bikers, truckers, hunters and all the other folks that she's met and fallen in love with over the years. Sometimes she writes urban romance and sometimes its aliens crash landing near a roadside bar. When she isn't writing, or wandering somewhere outdoors, she can often be found curled up with a good book and a kitty on her lap.

Read more at https://layladorine13.wixsite.com/layladorineauthor.